DON'T FORGET ME

DON'T FORGET ME

B.C.SCHILLER
Translated by Annette Charpentier

THOMAS & MERCER

Previously published as *Böses Geheimnis* by Edition M in Luxembourg in 2019. Translated from German by Annette Charpentier. First published in English by Thomas & Mercer in collaboration with Amazon Crossing in 2019.

Published by Thomas & Mercer, in collaboration with Amazon Crossing, Seattle

www.apub.com

Amazon, the Amazon logo, Thomas & Mercer and Amazon Crossing are trademarks of Amazon.com, Inc., or its affiliates.

ISBN-13: 9781542009638
ISBN-10: 1542009634

Cover design by Emma Rogers

Printed in the United States of America

First edition

'Lips that lie kill the soul'

(Proverb)

1

'I'm sorry!'

Five years ago, to the day, since her life disintegrated. Five years ago, to the day, since her husband and their little daughter disappeared. Five years ago, to the day, since her life stopped.

Olivia Hofmann knew what to expect when she approached the letterbox. She hesitated a few seconds and then opened it. She hoped it would be empty. At the same time, she hoped she did have mail. Should she open it or should she walk past? Ignore it? It sounded so easy but it wasn't. Not today of all days. The anniversary. And as on every anniversary, the card was lying on top of the mail. As always, there was no stamp. As always, the image on the front brought tears to her eyes. As always, she grabbed the card and ran upstairs. Olivia unlocked the door to her flat, sat down at the desk in her study and opened the bottom drawer. She glanced at the four other postcards. Four years, four postcards. Slowly she placed the fifth on top of the others. She read the words that she knew by heart:

'I'm sorry.'

Only one sentence. For the past five years Olivia had received these handwritten postcards.

It was all the unknown sender ever had to say.

'I'm sorry too,' Olivia said.

For how many more years would she receive these cards? For as long as she lived? With the tip of her shoe she kicked the drawer closed, banished the cards from sight and shut down that part of her memory.

There was now only blackness – a hole that contained neither questions nor answers. An icy black sun that lit up once a year, illuminating a bitter truth, shining a bright light on the facts without giving any answers.

Five years ago, to the day, since her husband Michael and their daughter Juli disappeared from Olivia's life.

2

The man's skin looked unhealthy. It had a reddish tint. His wide-open mouth was distorted into a ghoulish grimace, the lips caked with a residue of dried foam. The man's crooked fingers pointed upwards like spider's legs.

'This poor fellow went through a long struggle before finally losing his life. His murderer had administered potassium cyanide. Death takes between fifteen minutes and an hour,' Levi Kant said. Slowly he walked around the steel table on which the body lay. 'Anything you notice about the corpse?' The students around the table were pale-faced.

Levi was fifty-five years old and a lecturer at the police academy. He had once been the chief of the serious crime squad, but a bullet had abruptly ended his career. He'd refused to take early retirement and so they'd shuffled him off to this position as lecturer. This afternoon the students were having a practical lesson in pathology. Levi was very fond of practical work. It could be quite revealing, showing which of the students might be suitable for a future career in solving murders.

'I just want your first impressions,' Levi said. The students seemed embarrassed, glancing at one another nervously. The large room had a low ceiling and was brightly lit. A noisy fan on the wall sucked in cold air from the outside, but Levi noticed beads of sweat forming on the brows of some of the students. 'Can anyone tell me anything about the dead man?' Levi said.

'He was poisoned,' someone ventured at last.

'Ah, who would have guessed!' Levi said. 'Of course, it was poison, as I have already mentioned. I'd like more of an in-depth analysis.'

'The murderer was not a professional,' another student ventured.

'And why not?' Levi sounded more interested.

'I'd have done it with liquid prussic acid to cause instant death.'

'Sensitive soul, are you? What if the murderer was a sadist and wanted to see his victim suffer?' Levi said. 'With a lethal dose of prussic acid, death occurs within seconds after two or three breaths.' Levi patted the cold skin with his palm. 'This man here doubled up with pain and dropped to his knees. He crawled across the floor on all fours and vomited several times. His subconscious told him he was dying but his body wanted to live.'

Levi unbuckled the rubber strap of his watch and held it up. 'Let's assume the victim lived for another two minutes,' he said. 'It starts off with heartburn. The heart begins to beat like crazy. Cold sweat all over the body. The breathing gets more difficult. You vomit bile, and only then does your heart stop. That lasts two minutes, but what if this man fought his death for a full half hour?' Levi stopped and looked around. 'You need to develop empathy with the victim, feel their pain and suffering. Only then can you develop a cast-iron determination to catch the person who did it.'

'That's horrible,' mumbled one of the students, turning his back and retching.

Levi glowered at the young man. 'How will you catch the perpetrator if you close your eyes to the victim?' he asked. 'Turn around!'

'I don't think this is the right job for me,' the student whispered and rushed off for the exit. In his panic he bumped against a table and a limp arm slid out from under the sheet.

'Watch out or the dead will follow you!' Levi shouted after the man, then turned back to the other students. 'At the same time, you have to keep a lid on your own emotions and not let them affect your analytical judgement in the course of an investigation.'

Levi propped himself discreetly against the steel table. The old injury from the bullet hurt when he had to stand for a long time, but he was able to conceal this now. With a little luck and a lot of determination, combined with many hours of exercise, he could now walk without a limp. No way did he want his students to feel pity for him or consider him disabled.

'Now let's focus on the perpetrator,' Levi said. His angular face with its grey beard was mirrored in the polished surface of the steel table. 'What conclusions are we able to draw?'

'The perpetrator was presumably a woman.'

'What makes you assume that?'

'Women prefer to kill by poisoning.'

'OK. What else?'

'I'm guessing it wasn't done in the heat of the moment.' Another student stepped forward between the others.

'Interesting,' Levi said.

'Women tend to be more devious and subtle when planning a crime,' the student continued.

'There is one other great difference,' Levi said. 'Men mostly commit a murder in order to dominate. Women murder to escape oppression. Women frequently kill for self-protection, meaning they commit a murder in order to survive. That's the reason why such cases often happen in the home.'

'Which also means that victim and perpetrator most probably knew each other.'

Levi nodded and looked around. 'A dead body can give us all sorts of information. We're looking for a perpetrator who knew his or her victim. That means we need to closely investigate the family, friends and acquaintances.'

His mobile beeped.

'OK, that's the end of today's practical. Next week we'll move on to forensics and learn how to analyse the findings. How to identify an incinerated body.'

The students left the path lab but Levi stayed on a while in the gloomy basement room. He thought of the corpses waiting to be examined by the forensic pathologists. He couldn't count the number of times he'd been here in the course of his investigations, nor how often when viewing a body, he'd sworn not to give up until the murderer was caught. He had loved his job and missed his former life with a passion.

'Levi Kant. What a surprise!'

Levi jumped. It was the voice of Grünberg, the forensic pathologist, a man he'd often worked with in the old days.

'What brings you to our dark catacombs?' Grünberg asked.

'A practical lesson with my students,' Levi said. 'Part of the curriculum.'

'Ah, and you chose the poison victim for that?' Grünberg pointed to the half-covered body. 'An open-and-shut case – most likely the wife.'

'Well, that remains to be proved,' Levi said, 'though frankly I couldn't care less. I'm not chasing baddies any more.'

'Your clear-up rate was always spectacular,' Grünberg said, patting Levi on the shoulder, 'other than on your last case, though you gave it your very best.'

'I don't know what you mean,' Levi said, although he knew perfectly well what Grünberg was talking about.

'Lisa Manz, the girl who was burned to death,' Grünberg said. 'I still sometimes think of the charred body lying here on the table. A dreadful sight. Do you think about her sometimes too?'

'Nope. For me, the case is closed. I'm out.' Levi tapped his forehead with his finger. It was a lie. Of course, he often thought about that case. His failure to find Lisa Manz's murderer had been a low point in his life. It was five years ago, but he still couldn't come to terms with the decisions of his then superiors.

'How is your leg, by the way?' Grünberg changed the subject abruptly.

'It's nearly completely healed – I barely feel a twinge these days. I'll be able to run a marathon soon,' Levi joked, even though he was glad to be able to walk at all.

'I'm happy to hear it.' Grünberg's fingers stroked the poisoned body on the steel table. 'You could have ended up in a wheelchair.'

'Yes, I was very lucky.' Levi's jaw tightened as he tried not to remember. He'd acted like a complete amateur at the time.

Grünberg looked at him with sympathy. 'Do you fancy a coffee?'

'No, thanks,' Levi said. 'Stuff to do – need to correct some student essays.'

'I never saw you ending up as a teacher.'

'Well, life sometimes takes an unexpected turn,' Levi said, pushing away from the table. 'Have to go. Nice to catch up with you.'

He headed quickly for the door, his back straight but racked with sudden pain.

3

The patient was acting differently from normal. Something wasn't right. He was nervous and avoided looking her in the eye. All of a sudden and quick as lightning, the man grabbed the plastic bag at his feet and pulled something out.

'Lisa has come back.'

'What do you mean?' Olivia Hofmann asked. She was a psychiatrist and Jonathan Stade was her patient. 'I asked you a question.' She looked at Jonathan, waiting.

He was staring at her desk as if looking for something, but Olivia's desk was bare – no papers, no laptop, no lamp, not even a pen. Nothing to distract her patients. They were to focus their attention entirely on their inner lives.

'I took a photo of Lisa today.' Jonathan held the object towards Olivia. Only now did she recognise that it was a mobile phone in a colourful case.

'Jonathan, since when have you owned a mobile again?' In her head, Olivia quickly went through her notes from previous sessions. Jonathan Stade liked to expose himself in front of young girls and then take photos of their horrified faces on his mobile to enjoy later. Like many of her patients the clinic had referred him to Olivia's private practice after he'd done a stint in residential care there, and the state paid his fees. Barely any of Olivia's handful of friends could understand why she would work with patients like Jonathan who had a dark past and might be dangerous.

'But psychopaths have a soul too,' was her standard answer. It prevented further questions. She was suddenly overcome with fear and looked up from her thoughts to realise that Jonathan was staring at her.

'Do you want to see the photo?' he asked, holding the mobile out towards her.

'Yes, show it to me,' Olivia said, her tone neutral. She always strove to remain non-judgmental towards her clients. There was little to see in the photo. She could just about make out a shabby red rucksack in the foreground of a darkish room. Behind it stood a person, the face blurred and in profile. Olivia thought it might be a woman, but then again, she could have been mistaken.

'So this is Lisa?' Olivia said, handing the mobile back to Jonathan. 'Where did she come back from?'

'From hell. She's been dead a long time.'

'Oh, she's dead.' Olivia leaned forward. 'What happened to her?'

'Somebody burned her to death.' Jonathan swallowed hard, then continued. 'Lisa Manz was a beautiful girl. Not like the others . . .' He moved his arm in a wide circle, as if to embrace all the other girls in the world. 'Lisa was totally different.'

'In what way?'

'Lisa was an angel. She died in a fire, but now she's back. I've seen her.' Jonathan was waving his hands around and becoming more and more agitated.

'Calm down, Jonathan. Was Lisa your friend?'

'No, unfortunately not. She only had eyes for someone else.'

'How did you know her?'

'She was in the same clinic as me.'

'Was she ill?'

'No, not as ill as I was. Lisa's illness was different. And I really liked to look at her.' He picked up his woolly hat and kneaded it, embarrassed.

Olivia looked at him sceptically. Jonathan had probably watched this Lisa girl because she'd seemed an ideal victim, but it also seemed that something had happened between the two, or else Jonathan wouldn't be this nervous.

'How do you know the person in the photo is Lisa?' Olivia asked.

Jonathan felt in the pocket of his parka and pulled out an ornate pendant. It was in complete contrast to the shabby leather strap from which it hung. 'Lisa always wears this around her neck. It's her talisman.'

'Where did you get this?'

'It was in Lisa's rucksack. Take it – please!' Jonathan threw the necklace onto Olivia's desk. 'I can't keep it. It frightens me.'

Olivia looked at it, weighing it in her hand. It was heavy, probably solid silver. The engraving was intricate and unusual: two entwined snakes whose heads, in profile, touched as if kissing. Each snake had a ruby-red eye that glimmered maliciously and seemed to follow the movements of whoever was looking at it. Jonathan was right – it was spooky.

'Could you please show me the photo again?' she asked. Jonathan passed her his mobile. 'Why did this person not take the rucksack with her?'

'Lisa ran away from me. She's afraid she'll have to go back to hell,' Jonathan said.

'And where is this rucksack now?'

'I took it,' Jonathan answered, a bit calmer now. 'It's safe at my house.'

'Why don't you bring the rucksack to our next appointment?'

'But that won't be for another week. It'll be much too late.' Jonathan looked panic-stricken. 'She'll find me.'

'Lisa?'

'Yes, she'll just turn up, and it'll all start again,' Jonathan said. 'You have to help me.'

Olivia pondered a while, watching her patient. What kind of life, what kind of relationship might this man have if he weren't suffering from a psychological disorder of such severity? Lost in thought, she stroked the pendant on her desk. 'OK, I'll come and see you tomorrow, and you can show me this rucksack.'

Jonathan's face brightened. 'You're a good person, Doctor Hofmann.'

'Don't flatter me,' Olivia said, glancing at her watch. 'Our session is over. I'll see you tomorrow at nine o'clock at your house.'

Once Jonathan had left, Olivia took her laptop from the middle drawer of her desk and typed the name 'Lisa Manz' into the search engine. A list of articles popped up dating back five years.

'Daughter of surgeon Richard Manz butchered,' read one tabloid headline. 'The police have no fresh leads in the murder of fourteen-year-old Lisa Manz. The incinerated remains of the girl were found in a quarry near Lake Neusiedel. Several suspects have been released after extensive questioning. So far there is no trace of the murderer.'

4

Olivia's office was in a renovated nineteenth-century house in Vienna's Ninth District. From her window she had a wonderful view over a small park and during her lunch breaks would often sit and watch people enjoying themselves out there. Today, however, Olivia spent her break thinking about Jonathan and his connection with the dead girl, Lisa. She had tried drawing her patient out with gentle probing, but without much success. Scrolling through various online pieces about the horrific murder of the young girl, she came across the name of a journalist she knew.

'Anna wrote a whole feature on the case,' Olivia muttered to herself. Grabbing her phone she called Anna's number, but her mobile was off so she tried the office. 'I'd like to speak to Anna Hauser, the crime reporter?'

'I'm sorry, but Frau Hauser is not at her desk at the moment,' the girl from the switchboard said.

'Any idea where I could find her?' Olivia asked.

'I'm not sure she's available,' the girl said with some hesitation.

'It's urgent,' Olivia said. 'I'm a good friend.'

'OK then . . .' the girl replied reluctantly. 'Well, normally she has her lunch in the Schöne Perle.'

Olivia looked at her watch. It was nearly one o'clock and her next client wasn't due for another three hours, so she had enough time to cycle to the Second District. It was worth a try at least. Rushing out of the office, she hopped on her bike and set off.

Chaining her bike to a lamp post in front of the pub, Olivia walked the few steps towards the entrance. Fashionably furnished with retro 1960s furniture, the Schöne Perle was a popular place, although to Olivia's eyes it looked a little like a railway station. Looking around, she immediately spotted Anna sitting at one of the long wooden tables, reading a newspaper.

'Hi, Anna,' Olivia said, not waiting for an invitation to sit.

'Olivia! What are you doing here?' Anna looked pleased, one hand pushing her longish hair from her face. The two women had been at university together, and then had met up again following the death of Anna's mother. Since then, their acquaintance had deepened into a close friendship.

Olivia came quickly to the point. 'I need some information.'

'Yes, of course, if I can help you. What's it about?'

'Five years ago you wrote an article about the murder of Lisa Manz.'

'Yes, I remember,' Anna said, looking serious. 'It was all over the papers. They never caught the murderer. That was the story that made my name as a journalist. Didn't it happen around the same time as the tragedy in your own family?'

'Maybe,' Olivia replied vaguely. 'Tell me about the case.'

'Why do you want to know about it?' Anna looked at Olivia sharply.

'A client of mine mentioned Lisa Manz in a session,' Olivia said.

'One of your clients? How peculiar. Did he have anything to do with the case at the time?'

'No, not at all.'

'What's his name?' Anna's journalistic curiosity was clearly piqued.

'I can't tell you that. Anyway, I'm just interested. The only articles I can find online are pretty superficial, so I thought you might be able to give me a few more details. Your pieces were more in-depth than the others.' Olivia's compliment was deliberate.

'Lisa was the daughter of the surgeon, Richard Manz, and Theresa Manz, who used to be an actress.'

'I read that. Do you have anything else on Lisa?'

'She had behavioural problems and had been in psychiatric institutions several times. She was sectioned again after a more serious incident.'

'What kind of incident?'

'She attacked someone, but that's just between you and me. I got the information from one of my contacts. Everyone else at the time hid behind privacy and data protection laws.'

'Understandably. A well-known family like that doesn't want their daughter's mental health problems splashed all over the papers,' Olivia said.

'You're probably right, but the case was far more complicated and mysterious than that.' Anna leaned across and whispered conspiratorially, 'Lisa disappeared from the secure ward of the clinic, but it wasn't noticed for several days. They never called the police.'

'No way!' Olivia shook her head. The psychiatric clinic where she worked part-time also had a secure ward. It would be impossible to simply disappear from there. 'Someone must have helped her.'

'There were no signs. Nobody seemed to have noticed a thing.' Anna shrugged. 'A week later Lisa's body was found in the Burgenland, in the quarry at Sankt Margarethen, burned beyond all recognition. Tragically, many years before, her mother played the title role in *Medea* in Sankt Margarethen.'

'Did the parents identify her?' Olivia hesitated to ask. She tried to imagine what it must have been like for the parents to see the charred body of their child. An absolute horror.

'That was not necessary . . . nor possible. The police had to resort to dental records, which proved beyond doubt that the dead girl was Lisa Manz.'

'So the poor girl was burned to death. When I looked her up, I found that the search for the murderer went nowhere.'

'You can say that again.' Anna looked appalled. 'Someone called a halt to the investigation, if you ask me, but how can you prove something like that? There was a special unit on the case to begin with, but after a few dead ends the search was abandoned.'

'Were there any suspects or promising leads?'

'Of course there were a few suspects, but nothing led anywhere.'

'What makes you think the investigation was halted?' Olivia asked.

'Well, nobody bothered to find out how she managed to escape from the secure ward, and nobody seemed interested either in where she spent the days leading up to her death. Not even her own parents.'

'Seriously? They didn't want to know what had happened to their daughter?'

'She was a difficult girl – maybe they were glad she'd disappeared from their lives. Anyway, that was my gut feeling. A strange couple. A former actress and her husband, a surgeon who seemed to show no feeling at all,' Anna said.

'Do you have any idea where Lisa was hiding after her escape?'

'One of my contacts on the drug scene said she stayed for a short time in an empty property.'

'Who led the investigation?' Olivia asked.

'The chief inspector of the murder squad was a man called Levi Kant,' Anna said. 'I interviewed him at the beginning of the investigation. He seemed confident that he'd catch the perpetrator without too much trouble.'

'How wrong he was.'

'You can say that again.' Anna smiled. 'Levi used to keep me informed on homicide cases. He was a stubborn and persistent man who never gave up and I think he was close to catching the perpetrator.'

'Do you think I could talk to him?' Olivia got out her notebook to write down the name: Levi Kant.

'He's not with the murder squad any more,' Anna said.

'Was he transferred?'

'No.'

'Is he retired?'

'He could have taken early retirement, but instead he asked for a transfer to the police academy. It's been a long time since I last heard from him.'

'You said he was very close to solving the case. How come it didn't happen?'

'He was shot while arresting another criminal. He was in a coma for weeks and nearly died. Once he'd recovered, he never returned to the murder squad. After that the special unit was disbanded, and nobody cared about the Lisa Manz case any longer.'

'And you didn't find that suspicious?' Olivia asked Anna in surprise. She knew what a conscientious journalist her friend was.

'Obviously, we all had our theories that someone at the top had put a stop to the investigation. Whatever the reason, the fact remains that the Lisa Manz case went cold – like so many others.'

5

The old man shuffled through the living room and spread both arms. 'Flora! At last you're back! I've missed you so much.' His wrinkly face was beaming, and the corners of his eyes were moist. 'Flora,' he whispered.

'Papa, it's me. Olivia, your daughter.' She embraced her father and carefully led him back to his armchair. Olivia was not surprised at the greeting. Aside from the fact that her father was suffering from Alzheimer's she had inherited her Brazilian mother's looks – as well as her temperament.

'Olivia?' Her father raised his eyebrows in surprise and cleared his throat. 'Sorry, it was only a dream. I nodded off. I mistook you for her.'

'Of course you did, Papa.' Tenderly Olivia stroked her father's face, then she sat down on the arm of his chair. Leopold Hofmann was in his late sixties and, until five years ago, had worked as a psychiatrist in private practice in Vienna, until Alzheimer's set in and he became more and more confused. Eventually he'd had to give up work.

At the time Michael and Juli had just disappeared and Olivia had been at the lowest point of her life.

How often she thought of that day.

She'd come home from work earlier than usual and was looking forward to giving Juli her surprise.

'Where's my present, Mummy?' Juli had shouted, clapping her hands with joy and jumping up and down until her little face went pink.

'Daddy has your surprise. Come on quickly to the bathroom now, and after your bath you can put on your lovely pink frilly dress.'

She'd gone into the living room and stopped short at the sight of her husband, Michael, lying on the sofa, staring into the distance with glazed eyes.

'Is everything OK? Did you get the present for Juli? You know, the blonde Barbie with the red raincoat?'

'Everything's OK. I just had a headache and a few black thoughts,' Michael said.

'Please, pull yourself together for once. Let's just be a happy family today,' Olivia said.

'Promise. We belong together forever, my darling.' He got up from the sofa and gave her a fleeting peck on the cheek.

◆ ◆ ◆

'We belong together forever.' The sentence still echoed around Olivia's head. How often had she wondered whether she'd overlooked something in Michael's behaviour. As a psychiatrist, should she have noticed anything?

Her father mumbled a few words, bringing her back to the present. He was the only family she had left and she didn't want to lose him as well. For that reason, a nursing home was not an option. Maybe it was selfish, but she wanted Leopold to stay in his own house.

'Have you taken your medication?' Olivia asked. She knew from experience that medical people never followed medical advice.

'Of course.' Leopold nodded and got up as quickly as he could. On his good days, he was a handsome man, with his grey hair, weathered face and blue eyes. 'Three blue ones daily, and a white one in the evening. The yellow one in the morning. I'm not suffering from dementia yet.' He smiled at her conspiratorially.

'Oh, Papa!' Olivia sighed and went into the kitchen to heat up a frozen meal in the microwave. As the nurse only stayed until early afternoon, Olivia had disconnected the electric hob, the oven and the water heater. It prevented Leopold from injuring himself or inadvertently setting the flat on fire.

'It happened again today,' Olivia said when they sat down to dinner.

'What did?' Her father forked through his spaghetti without much enthusiasm.

'I got another postcard.'

'How lovely. From Flora?'

'Mama is dead!' Olivia said with unusual anger. She regretted it immediately when she saw the tears well up in her father's eyes.

'That's so very sad,' Leopold said. 'Flora is dead. I won't talk about her any more.'

'What I wanted to say,' Olivia started again, 'was that I received a postcard from Marrakech today. Nonsense, only the picture was of Marrakech,' she corrected herself. 'Somebody wanted to remind me of that day five years ago. You know what I mean.'

'Five years ago to the day since my granddaughter Juli disappeared. You didn't look after her properly,' Leopold said. He pushed the spaghetti around his plate. The food was cold already.

'Not exactly top-notch cuisine, is it?' Olivia got up to take the plates to the kitchen.

'We share the same fate,' she heard her father mumble from the living room. 'Suddenly our loved ones disappear and here we are, all alone.'

'There's no comparison. You led a wonderful life with Mama, but I had only a few years of happiness.' Olivia knew there was no sense in arguing with her father. Her mother had been so full of verve and energy that her sudden death from a stroke six years earlier had been a complete shock from which her father had never recovered. And now he was ill and spending more and more time in a world of his own.

Olivia helped her father lie down on the sofa and watched him take the right tablets. The depressing scene reminded her again of Jonathan and the conversation about the murdered Lisa Manz. According to Jonathan, the girl had once stayed at the psychiatric clinic where Olivia herself worked two days a week. Her father had also worked there at one time. It was peculiar how similarly their careers had developed.

On the off-chance that he might remember her, she asked, 'Papa, do you happen to recall a girl called Lisa Manz? She was in your clinic for treatment. Probably about five years ago. You should know her, really. Does the name ring a bell?'

But her dad seemed to have drifted off into his own world again, because there was no reaction. Instead, with trembling hands, he turned on the DVD of an old film by Werner Herzog, where Klaus Kinski pulls a large boat up a steep hill. Leopold had seen this film about a hundred times before but even so he was always fascinated by the story and he concentrated on it as if it were the first time. He particularly loved the scenes showing the mighty Amazon River, which he'd often travelled up with Flora.

Olivia had put on her coat and was giving her father a quick kiss on the cheek, when he grabbed her arm and whispered, 'Of course I know Lisa Manz. She was a very sad and very difficult girl.'

6

That night, Olivia tossed and turned, her sleep disturbed by dreams of Lisa Manz. She'd found only a single photo of Lisa on the Internet, but couldn't imagine this gentle-faced, elfin girl with the dreamy eyes as being difficult. But then photos could be deceptive, as Olivia knew all too well.

'It's not what you're thinking.' Lisa's gentle voice invaded her dreams, her fingers tenderly stroking Olivia's head. 'Please help me.'

'But you're dead,' Olivia answered.

'Who knows?' Lisa answered sadly. Then she offered Olivia her hand and they walked together through a dark and dingy house, empty and ready for demolition, where two bicycles were leaning against a wall. 'We need to look for him,' Lisa said, mounting one of the bikes.

'Who are we looking for?'

'Wait and see. We'll confront him and find out all the answers.'

Olivia jumped on her saddle, and they sped off through the dark city streets.

'Where are we going to look for him?' Olivia asked.

'In his favourite place,' Lisa answered. Suddenly she burst into flames, turning into a column of fire.

Olivia woke with a start, her heart pounding. She was still caught up in the dream and the image of Lisa burning.

Unable to go back to sleep, she got up and went over to her desk, then began to write down everything she remembered. Jonathan had claimed that Lisa had returned, but the girl had been burned beyond all recognition – she could not possibly have survived. But what if everything was different from how it seemed?

◆ ◆ ◆

In the morning, Olivia felt drained and considered cancelling her appointment with Jonathan, but then remembered the panic in his eyes – he needed her. With a sigh she set up the coffee machine and went to have a cold shower. Finally, after two strong espressos, she felt better and got on her bike.

The block of flats where Jonathan Stade lived was outside the Inner Ring, in the Tenth District of Favoriten. It looked shabby. The windows of the shop on the ground floor were boarded up, and even the neon sign had been removed, although one could still see 'Hosiery' written on the grey wall.

She was walking towards the entrance when a top-floor window ripped open and Jonathan's head appeared. He leaned outside with such a jerk that his flat cap fell off and sailed downwards.

'Hi, Jonathan,' Olivia called to him. 'Here I am.'

Jonathan immediately disappeared into the room behind, as if Olivia's voice had frightened him.

'I'm coming up now,' Olivia called anyway, but got no reply.

In the flat upstairs someone uttered a loud cry. It was Jonathan's voice. The morning sun shone brightly on the front of the house and Olivia had to shade her eyes to see more clearly. Jonathan was again leaning out of the window, stammering and confused. Olivia couldn't make any sense of it.

'Stay calm, Jonathan,' Olivia called up to him. 'I'm coming.'

Jonathan froze for a moment, his long hair whipped upwards by a gust of wind, making it appear from below as though smoke was rising from his shrivelled head.

'Jonathan, what's the matter?'

'Help!' Jonathan shouted. 'They want to take the rucksack.'

'Who wants to do that?'

'I don't know.' Jonathan seemed to want to say something else, but then he suddenly disappeared inside.

'Jonathan, close the window and count to a hundred!' Olivia shouted. Jonathan was in crisis. If he broke down now, it could have very bad consequences, Olivia thought.

Suddenly, Jonathan was standing on the window ledge, swaying as he stared down, his arms waving. There was a shadow behind him. Olivia wasn't sure, but it could have been a hand giving him a push. For a couple of seconds Jonathan wobbled, desperately trying to keep his balance, until slowly, inevitably, he fell. Olivia froze. She could neither cry nor move. She stared as Jonathan's body spun once. She saw his wide-open eyes. The mouth forming the word 'Lisa'. A fraction of a second later he crashed to the concrete. A pool of blood spread quickly under his head, glistening in the sunlight.

'Oh my God, I'll call an ambulance!' Olivia shouted, battling the shock. With trembling fingers, she punched the number of the emergency services into her mobile.

Then she knelt down next to Jonathan, feeling for his pulse, but he was beyond help. Stunned, she glanced up at the window to see a shadow move away from the opening. Without a doubt, there was somebody else in Jonathan's flat.

She sprang to her feet and raced towards the block of flats, hit by a waft of musty air as she pushed open the heavy front door.

'Hello, is anybody there?' she called into the dark entrance hall and up the staircase. A door slammed somewhere upstairs, just as the front door fell shut behind her with a loud squeak of the hinges. Suddenly she was shrouded in darkness and she groped for a light switch. A dim light flickered on as she entered the glass-sided lift. With a jerk, the old-fashioned mechanism started its journey upwards. Hurried steps echoed on the staircase and through the frosted glass she could see a blurred figure running down the stairs. Frantically she tried to stop the lift, but the button would not respond. After what felt like an eternity, she finally reached the top floor. There were only two doors. On one of them was a piece of paper with the name 'Stade'.

The door to Jonathan's flat stood ajar and Olivia ran into the room with the open window. A light gust of wind blew away the musty smell. She squinted against the bright sun and looked down. Four floors below she could see the strangely distorted body of Jonathan on the concrete. No one was running away. Several people were rushing towards the body, and two policemen had already arrived and were pushing the onlookers back. Someone pointed upstairs. Hearing an ambulance siren on its way, Olivia instinctively stepped back from the window. The lift was called to the ground floor and with a groan started moving downwards.

Slowly she retreated into the room, trying to get her thoughts in order – and to suppress a rising panic. There was no doubt about it; she'd seen the shadow of a person behind Jonathan and a hand pushing him out of the window. She cursed herself for not having arrived earlier. Maybe Jonathan would still be alive.

She looked around the room. It was a living room with old-fashioned furniture – a beige three-piece suite and a coffee table with a smoked glass top. A large rubber tree stood against the back wall, extending its branches over the sofa. The walls were covered with prints of landscapes in heavy gilt frames and a TV magazine lay on the table. The television on the dark brown sideboard was not plugged in. The room was spotless with not a speck of dust, and nor did there seem to be any personal items belonging to

Jonathan. Something in this sad room was bothering her, although she couldn't put her finger on it straight away. Then she realised: it was the utter tidiness of the place. There was nothing to indicate that there'd been a fight. She stepped into the hall, lost in thought.

'Stay where you are!' Two policemen blocked Olivia's way. 'Who are you? Do you know the dead person? Do you live here?'

She searched in her bag for her ID card. 'My name is Dr Olivia Hofmann. I'm Jonathan Stade's psychiatrist. No, I don't live here.'

'What are you doing here?' one of the policemen asked.

'I had an appointment with my client. He wanted to show me something.'

'What did he want to show you?'

'A rucksack he'd found.'

'A rucksack? Are you kidding us?'

'Of course not. Apparently the rucksack belonged to a girl who was murdered five years ago.'

The policeman pushed his cap back and rubbed his forehead. 'What was the name of this murdered girl?' he asked.

'Lisa Manz.'

'Never heard of her.'

'Just a moment.' His colleague looked at Olivia. 'You wait here. I know someone who has never forgotten Lisa Manz.'

7

Sitting in his office in the police academy, Levi Kant yawned. He'd been working his way through the essays by the police cadets since early morning, but the pile of papers was not getting any smaller. He glanced out of the window, taking in the uninspiring view of the tram station. Today a man was sitting in the shelter throwing breadcrumbs to the pigeons.

That could have been me, Levi thought, *if I'd taken up the offer of early retirement.*

His wife, Rebecca, would never have allowed it, however. She'd urged him to quit the police and take on the job as a lecturer. 'It's fate. You have to change your life,' she'd said. After the accident, he'd been trapped in a black hole of depression for weeks and had turned more and more cynical. Rebecca had found it increasingly difficult to bear and had given him a choice: either he left the police and took up the post as lecturer or their marriage was over. And that was why he was sitting here now, marking essays.

The phone interrupted his thoughts.

'Can I help?'

'Is that Chief Inspector Levi Kant?'

'Not Chief Inspector any more. I'm a lecturer these days,' Levi said, suddenly alert.

'We have a body and a woman who knew the victim.'

A wave of alarm went through him. 'OK, and why are you ringing me?'

'It's about a rucksack that allegedly belonged to a certain Lisa Manz. Who five years ago . . .'

'I know. It was me who dealt with that case,' Levi said, interrupting the policeman. 'Give me the address. I'll be right there.'

After his accident Levi had asked his colleagues to inform him straight away if any new information turned up on the Lisa Manz case, but in five years nothing whatsoever had happened. Now, as he opened the door to his office, he shot one last look at the pile of papers on his desk. He'd wasted enough time here.

A short time later he parked his Saab 900 Turbo convertible in a side street near the block of flats. Ducking under the police cordon set up on the pavement, he glanced briefly at the outline chalked on the concrete and the dried pool of blood.

'Keep out, please.' A policeman approached him. Levi was about to explain himself when a man in plain clothes appeared at the entrance to the block of flats.

'It's OK,' he said, before turning to Levi. 'I knew you'd turn up here.'

'Hello, Reiter. I had a call from a colleague.'

'Levi, my God!' Inspector Reiter rolled his eyes. 'You simply can't let it go, can you?'

'It's how I'm made,' Levi replied. 'What actually happened here?'

Reiter quickly put him in the picture. 'If you ask me, it's all very simple. Someone hears voices telling him to jump. Wouldn't be the first time it's happened.'

'Unless you have it all wrong about this particular incident. Can I speak to the witness?'

'Yes, but only briefly. Fourth floor, but I'd take the lift, mate, with that leg of yours.'

'Thanks for the tip.' Levi refused to be provoked and took the lift.

'Chief Inspector Levi Kant?' a young policeman asked.

'I'm not an inspector any more, but a lecturer at the academy,' Levi replied.

'Sorry,' the policeman said. 'I called you because the murder case was quite notorious at the time. I read all about it in the papers.'

'Where's the witness?'

'Here.' The policeman opened the door to a small room.

'Why am I being held?' the woman asked when Levi entered. She was slim, with short dark hair and sensual lips. Her pale green eyes flashed angrily.

'You mentioned a rucksack that might have belonged to Lisa Manz,' Levi said, ignoring her question.

'Maybe you'd better introduce yourself,' the woman said, folding her arms. 'Who are you?'

'My name is Levi Kant. Five years ago, I was the lead investigator on the Manz case. And who are you?'

'My name is Olivia Hofmann.'

She showed him her ID card. It confirmed what she'd said, only she looked considerably younger than the thirty-nine years printed on the card.

'I'm a psychiatrist. The dead man was my patient, Jonathan Stade. But it wasn't suicide – he was pushed.'

'Hold on,' Levi interrupted. 'You're talking murder here. What makes you say that?'

'I was downstairs on the pavement and I saw someone push Mr Stade out of the window. I told your colleagues all about it.'

'I'd like to hear it again. Can you describe the person?' Levi asked.

'No, but they fled down the stairs straight afterwards.'

'You must have seen something.' Levi's eyebrows rose sceptically. 'Was it a man or a woman?'

'No idea. I was on my way up in the lift. The sides of the lift are frosted glass.'

'Was your relationship with the victim more than just professional?'

'What do you mean?' Olivia was growing irritable.

'Home visits by psychiatrists are not the usual thing,' Levi stated.

'It was an emergency. The name of the dead man was Jonathan Stade, by the way. Please call him by his name and not just "the victim". It's so impersonal. Yes, he was my patient. I mentioned that.'

'Of course. Anything else?' Levi was walking into the hallway with Olivia when Reiter arrived with the forensics team.

'Hello, Levi,' a blonde woman said. Even in the white overalls she looked attractive. 'I thought you'd left our gang.'

'I lecture at the police academy now, but in my mind I never left,' he said. 'Katharina, could you take a close look at the windowsill and the frame? I want to know whether Stade tried to grab on somewhere – any little thing you notice that might indicate he actually could have been pushed.'

'Stop, Levi,' Reiter interrupted. 'This is my case. You can have a talk with the witness, but that's all.'

'OK, OK,' Levi conceded. 'I just wanted to help.'

'How very touching,' Reiter replied, following his team into the living room.

'What kind of emergency was it exactly?' Levi asked once he was alone with Olivia again.

Olivia told him about the red rucksack and the photo Jonathan had taken.

'Oh, so Jonathan Stade took a photo?' Levi said, giving her a questioning look.

'Yes, I saw it on his phone.'

Levi went to Reiter and asked, 'Has anyone found a mobile?'

'No, no mobiles here,' Reiter answered curtly.

'But we have just found a rucksack in case you're interested,' Katharina called from the living room.

'Where?'

'It was hidden in the wall.' Katharina said, pointing behind her. 'There's a large cavity, presumably from an old chimney. Seems our victim tucked the rucksack out of sight in there.'

'Can I have a look at it?' Levi felt the old thrill in every cell of his body. It told him he'd not become completely numb.

'Here you are. It has a smiley sticker with the initials LM on it.' Katharina passed him a large plastic evidence bag containing a red rucksack. Levi swallowed hard. When Lisa Manz disappeared, she'd been carrying a red rucksack with exactly this smiley sticker on it. It was Lisa's rucksack. Levi tried to open the plastic bag, but Reiter grabbed his hand.

'You're not a chief inspector any more, Levi,' he said. 'Go back to your students.'

'It's Lisa's rucksack.' Levi's voice was cracking.

'We'll investigate everything thoroughly, I promise. You can depend on us.' Reiter pushed Levi out into the hall. 'By the way, we also found this.' He showed Levi a sheet of paper, also sealed in a plastic bag.

The whole message was written in capital letters. 'LISA WAS AN ANGEL. I AM GUILTY.'

'Looks like a confession. What do you think?' Reiter put the evidence back in his folder. 'It does look like suicide.'

'Exactly.' Levi scratched his head and went back to Olivia, who was waiting in the corridor.

'We've found Lisa's rucksack and a piece of paper with a pre-sumed suicide note,' he said.

'And what are your thoughts on that?' Olivia slowly walked over to Levi. 'You believe Jonathan committed suicide, don't you?'

'It looks like it. We'll check it out.'

'But you're not a policeman any more. You failed your mission five years ago, and now you have a guilty conscience because Lisa's murderer is still free. That's the reason you're meddling with this now.'

'No, it's nothing like that,' Levi said.

'Sorry, it came out the wrong way,' Olivia said quietly, her shoulders suddenly drooping.

All of a sudden she looked like a little girl, her confidence evaporated, but at least she wasn't hurling accusations at him any more.

'Jonathan was my client. He was in therapy with me, and he was getting so much better,' she said.

'No one ever really knows what's going on in another person's head. Some people throw themselves in front of a train, others jump off bridges or, like here, out of a window. Suddenly their view of the world gets more and more limited, and they can't see any other way. Contrary to public opinion, it's particularly bad on a beautiful day,' Levi said in an effort to comfort Olivia.

'How do you know?' Olivia asked, looking at him steadily with her pale green eyes.

'I did a few terms of psychology.'

'You don't believe it was murder, do you? Listen, Jonathan wasn't suicidal. He had a new outlook on life, and it had helped him come out of the darkness into the light.'

'Like I said, my colleagues will investigate all of this,' Levi said. 'Shall I call you a taxi?'

'No, thanks. I came on my bike.'

'Oh right. Will you be OK?'

'Do I look that unfit?'

'It was a stupid question. I mean, of course, are you happy to cycle after what's just happened?'

'Yes. I find cycling relaxing. It helps me think things through.'

Levi pushed his hands deep into the pockets of his jeans, watching as Olivia, head lowered, walked off down the stairs. A psychiatrist on a bike, he mused. He hadn't been expecting that today.

8

A hunched or crouching position may indicate someone's extreme mental burden, even guilt, so Olivia tried to sit as upright as possible. 'One of my patients died today in terrible circumstances,' she said. 'I blame myself. I may have contributed to it.'

'Tell me what happened and why you think you might somehow be responsible,' Ulf Karlsson said in encouragement. Ulf was Swedish but had grown up in Austria.

After the conversation with Levi Kant, Olivia had rung Ulf to make an appointment. She'd known him since her university days, first as her tutor, then as her supervisor. In the past five years she'd spoken to him exclusively about her private tragedy. She'd tried to come to terms with the incomprehensible through talking about it, and step by step had found a way back to some kind of normality. Today, however, she'd come to his office to discuss a client.

'So you believe someone pushed Jonathan out of the window?' Ulf asked, folding his hands in his lap.

'Yes, I saw a shadow behind him. And when I went up in the lift, someone ran down the stairs.'

'And you're absolutely sure?'

'Yes, but it all happened so quickly, and I was still in shock.'

'Understandably.' Ulf closed his eyes briefly to reflect on what she'd said. Finally he said, 'Could it be a protective statement? You blame yourself for the death of a patient because your therapy hasn't helped him. You would find it far more bearable if someone had murdered him. You wouldn't then need to feel responsible.'

'But it wasn't like that.' Olivia involuntarily clenched her hands, but immediately relaxed her fingers when she saw the surprised expression on her supervisor's face. 'I didn't imagine it. Not even you believe me – it's driving me mad!' She told Ulf about the goals and targets she'd agreed with Jonathan. 'Someone with that kind of timetable, an agenda for life, doesn't kill himself. You must know that.'

'Yes, but sometimes people commit sudden irrational acts. And that is in no way your fault,' he said, trying to calm her down.

'But I feel terrible.'

'Why don't you write everything down and reflect on it again,' Ulf suggested. Then he abruptly changed the subject, asking, 'What about Michael and Juli?'

'Why do you mention them now?'

'Yesterday was *the* anniversary. Did you get another postcard?'

'Yes.' Olivia nodded and slumped in her chair. 'It was like falling into a deep black hole again.'

'Next time we'll talk about your loss.'

'Thank you. I'm so glad I can talk to you,' Olivia said, clutching a tissue, desperately trying not to cry in front of Ulf.

Olivia saw clients for the rest of the day, only finding time to relax as evening closed in. She took her notebook from the middle drawer of her desk and began to write down the main events of the day in brief sentences, as Ulf had suggested. Rereading her notes didn't help her disquiet – she needed to find out precisely what had happened but had no idea how to go about it. She delved into her pocket and pulled out the card the inspector had given her. After a moment's hesitation she called the number.

Inspector Reiter answered on the first ring, as if he'd been waiting for her call. 'Reiter here. What can I do for you?'

'Doctor Hofmann here. Any news on the Jonathan Stade case?' Olivia asked, knowing immediately that her question was incredibly naive. The police were not allowed to give out information. But she was wrong.

'Frau Hofmann, good of you to call. I looked again at your witness statement about the person you believe you saw in the window and on the stairs. There's not the slightest evidence that anyone else was there. No one apart from you saw anybody and there are no traces on the windowsill, nor on the frame, that could indicate a struggle.'

'But you found the rucksack. It's clear evidence that my client wasn't lying to me.'

'The rucksack did indeed belong to Lisa Manz.'

'Well then, I was right about that. Maybe Lisa is alive, and it was another girl who was murdered.' Olivia was getting upset.

'What do you mean?' Reiter said, trying to calm her. 'Lisa Manz was murdered five years ago. Her body was identified beyond all doubt. All of this was clearly proved.'

'But Jonathan saw a person who could be Lisa in some dark house and took a photo of her,' Olivia said, trying to keep the frustration from her voice.

'So you claim, but we haven't found any mobile.'

'What direction are your investigations taking now?' Olivia knew she sounded impatient. Once she was upset, she found it difficult to control her emotions.

'Frau Doctor Hofmann,' Reiter said, his tone formal and cool. 'Keep out of things that are not your business and leave us to do our job in peace. I'm not allowed to give you any more details about the case. Only what you know already from your own inquiries. When Lisa Manz was murdered five years ago, no perpetrator could be identified.'

'I know. Another cold case.'

'That's what they call them on TV. We call it Investigation Level Three.'

'Low priority, I assume.'

'Exactly. I did check the files, of course. There were several persons under suspicion at the time, and they were all interviewed. Jonathan Stade was one of them.'

'Jonathan was among the suspects?' Olivia was speechless. 'I didn't know that.'

'There was no evidence against him – then.'

'What do you mean?' Olivia had no idea where this conversation was going.

'In the next few days we expect to close the Lisa Manz case. We think we've found the murderer.'

Only now the penny dropped. 'You think Jonathan Stade murdered Lisa?'

'I'm not allowed to say any more,' Reiter said.

'Please! He was one of my patients. I was there when he died.'

'Sorry, not possible. You must understand my position. Look on the bright side – after five years we may finally have found the murderer.'

'Even though Jonathan's dead and can't defend himself?' Olivia asked in desperation.

'Yes, even though he's dead,' Reiter repeated. 'In short, Frau Doctor Hofmann, the case will be closed very soon.'

'So a cold case is turning into a closed case,' Olivia retorted sarcastically and ended the conversation. She knew she'd never be able to accept this. She also knew she had only one chance of clearing this up: the ex-policeman Levi Kant. She had to convince him that Lisa Manz's murderer was still free.

Only now did she remember the pendant Jonathan had given her to look after. Should she have told the police about it? Yes, certainly, but it would only have strengthened the inspector's belief that Jonathan was the murderer.

She turned back to her laptop and checked her emails. Aside from the usual newsletters and medical info there was an email from an unknown sender. No text, just an attachment. Olivia hesitated a moment before clicking on the file. A blurred photo appeared – the one Jonathan had claimed to be of Lisa.

9

Levi Kant was waiting at a street corner near the police headquarters, away from surveillance cameras. 'Have you got the photos?' he asked the blonde woman who walked up to him.

'Here, on the memory stick.' Katharina pulled the stick from her pocket. 'There are some photos of the red rucksack with the initials LM and shots of the dead Jonathan Stade from forensics.'

'Any evidence of external influence?'

'No, nothing, although we did find considerable traces of psychotropic drugs in his body. By the way, it wasn't easy to get this for you.'

'You're a star!' Levi gave Katharina a kiss on the cheek.

'You owe me one, Levi.'

'Maybe we can go out for dinner some time?' Levi looked at Katharina in anticipation.

'No, let's leave that – you're taken already. But hey, that witness made quite an impact on you, didn't she?'

'What do you mean?'

'Well, she's exactly your type,' Katharina said with a smirk.

'But I'm happily married.'

'I'm not so sure . . . Anyway, I need to get back.' Katharina gave Levi a pat on the shoulder. 'You look after yourself!'

'Well, you know, people like me have nine lives.'

Was that true? Levi *had* nearly died. He'd lost an enormous amount of blood and his heart had stopped. He didn't want to think about it any more. Ever since the shooting, he'd felt like a caged animal, like the living dead. He gave his lectures at the academy, worked regular hours and abstained from high-impact exercise, but he missed the rush of adrenalin he used to get when he came across a decent lead, or when he'd worked day and night with his team on a case. That had stopped abruptly, from one minute to the next. And now, Lisa Manz's rucksack had catapulted him back into that life. He had a goal again.

He went to the narrow road where he'd parked his Saab. The convertible purred along the streets of Vienna, attracting envious looks from other drivers, but Levi didn't notice – he was too busy contemplating his next move.

Soon he had left the city centre behind and was driving along the Höhenstrasse. Massive entrance gates on either side shielded mansions surrounded by enormous gardens. Levi stopped the car in front of an ornate wrought-iron gate and got out. A surveillance camera on the wall next to the gate followed his every move.

'Inspector Levi Kant,' he said in response to a distorted voice from the loudspeaker.

'On what matter?'

'I have new information about Lisa.'

Immediately the gate swung open, and Levi drove his car up a broad gravel driveway. The mansion reminded him of an oversized country residence. Beneath the wooden shingles of the steeply pitched roof hung the skull of a stag, complete with antlers. A balcony with an intricately carved railing ran the entire length of the first floor, while a curved set of steps led up to the entrance on the ground floor. Levi was expected.

'There's new information after five years of silence? I find that hard to believe.'

Levi knew this woman well – Theresa Manz, née von Stollwerk, Lisa's mother. Her ethereal, elfin beauty had scarcely changed over the past five years, although when she came down the steps to greet Levi, he noticed that she was swaying slightly.

'My daughter's death has done some damage to my career, but you're well aware of that,' she said regretfully.

What career? Levi thought. How awful it must have been for Lisa to live with a mother who seemed devoid of all emotion. She'd not called him once at the police headquarters to ask for information or progress on her daughter's case.

'I've brought a few photos I'd like you to have a look at,' Levi said, opening his folder.

'Ah, only photos?' Theresa dismissed it with a disappointed look. 'I thought you were bringing me the head of Lisa's murderer.'

'He could be in one of the photos,' Levi said.

'Come in,' Theresa said, taking Levi's arm. 'What happened to your leg?' she continued as he awkwardly climbed the steps.

'I overdid the jogging a little,' he said.

The entrance hall hadn't changed at all during the past five years. The stuffed polar bears and lions still guarded the place; on the walls, stuffed eagles with spread wings kept a watchful eye on their prey.

'Pretty scary,' Theresa said, noticing Levi glancing at the animals. 'I'd rather put the whole lot on a bonfire, but for Richard these are all symbols of his masculinity.'

'Isn't it your old family home?' Levi asked. He knew from the files that it was Theresa who had the money in this family.

'Yes, but if I throw out all this rubbish, it would be like castrating my husband.' Theresa laughed out loud. 'Let's go to the drawing room,' she said.

'And now show me the photos,' she ordered, sitting down on a huge sofa with a theatrical flourish. 'Would you join me in a drink?' she asked. 'Ah no, you're on duty.' She answered her own question.

'Is that Lisa's rucksack?' Levi asked, showing Theresa the first photo.

'Yes.' Theresa nodded, waving her hands excitedly. 'I recognise that thing. Lisa got it from one of those dreadful vintage shops you find everywhere these days. I hated that scruffy thing.'

'It is Lisa's rucksack then. You recognise it. Are you sure?'

'Of course I'm sure. It also has her initials, LM. I remember so clearly when she turned up with it. I was preparing for my role as Medea when she came bursting into the room and completely ruined all my concentration. Out of the window. She was such a demanding girl.'

'I think she was rather a lonely girl,' Levi said. He couldn't help himself.

'How do you mean?'

'Oh, nothing.' Levi quickly moved on, pulled out the picture of Jonathan Stade's body from his folder and put it on the table.

'Oh my God!' Theresa placed a hand in front of her mouth in faux horror. 'Who is that? Is the man dead?'

'We found Lisa's rucksack in this man's flat,' Levi informed her. 'Is he familiar to you?'

'No. Was he Lisa's friend?' Theresa asked in disgust. 'If he was, he was a bad choice.'

'No, the man was not Lisa's friend.'

'Is he her murderer?' Theresa fiddled with her jewellery nervously.

'It looks like it,' Levi answered. 'All the evidence points in his direction.'

Disappointed but not quite sure why, Levi collected the photos and put them back in the folder. What had he expected? That Theresa would look at Jonathan's photo and shriek, 'Yes, he was our gardener!'

'What's going on here?' A tall man with bushy eyebrows appeared in the doorway. His hair was thinner than five years ago, but the moustache was still neatly trimmed. Wearing short lederhosen and the traditional linen waistcoat, he perfectly matched the country-house style of his mansion. Without acknowledging Levi, he approached Theresa and stopped, his stance deliberately intimidating. 'What have you told him? None of your usual nonsense, I hope,' he hissed.

You haven't changed a single bit, Richard Manz, Levi thought. *You still want to control everything. Back then you were also constantly meddling with the investigation, calling up all your medical friends when you didn't like how something was going.*

'Herr Kant, what are you doing here?' Only now did he turn towards Levi, looking him up and down with open contempt.

'I just wanted to share our latest findings about the case with your wife,' Levi answered calmly.

'And in what capacity are you here, pray?' Richard Manz stuck out his chin, his hands buried in the pockets of his lederhosen. He was even carrying a short ornate knife with a staghorn handle in its special side pocket. Dressed in his Tyrolean costume, nothing but perfection would do.

'Not in an official capacity,' Levi replied honestly. 'But since I led the investigation at the time, I considered it my duty . . .'

'There was no need for it, Kant,' Manz interrupted him. 'I have the latest information. What's that?' he asked, pointing to the folder with the photos, still lying on the table.

'I asked your wife whether she knew the man in question,' Levi answered, taking the picture of Jonathan Stade out of the folder and handing it to the other man.

'So this is the man who murdered our daughter?' Manz said, squinting at the picture before dropping it as though it were poisoned. Slowly it sailed to the floor. 'What do the other photos show?' he asked, clicking his fingers impatiently.

'Lisa's rucksack,' Levi said.

'And . . . what about it?'

'I just wanted to ascertain whether this rucksack did indeed belong to your daughter.'

'But they all look the same,' Manz said, shrugging his shoulders.

'No, this ugly thing definitely belonged to our daughter,' Theresa chimed in.

'Well, she had your bad taste. You only ever deal with superficial things – another reason why your brain is so empty.'

'At least I don't have to kill defenceless animals to prove my masculinity,' Theresa hissed before getting up and going over to the bar in the corner.

'Stop bloody drinking!' Manz said.

'You can't boss me around any longer. All that is over and done with now.'

'You'll get the rucksack back once the case is closed,' Levi told them, heading for the door. He had no intention of watching them row.

'What did you say?' Manz appeared to have forgotten Levi was there.

'I said that you'll get the rucksack back,' Levi repeated.

'Burn it! I never want to see it again,' Manz said.

'But it's Lisa's rucksack!' Theresa propped herself on the sideboard. 'I want it here, with me.'

'I repeat: burn the rucksack, just like Lisa was burned.'

10

Lisa's diary

I'm terrified of horses, but I absolutely must not show it. I shake every time Mama takes me to the stables. Mama sits there with her friends, drinking tea to calm her nerves, while I stand in front of my horse as it paws the ground nervously. The trainer talks reassuringly to the animal and only then turns to me.

'Get up now, Lisa. This horse is very calm. You don't want to disappoint your father, do you?'

I sit on the horse and hold my breath. I only have to do a few circuits around the paddock then it'll all be over. If I fail again, the riding instructor will talk to Papa, I'm sure about that. I need to pull myself together.

'You're making the horse very nervous,' the teacher tells me. He's irritated and pulls at the long rein. The horse leaps forward and I can't keep my balance, so I slide forward and grab its mane. My feet lose their hold in the stirrups and I fall heavily to the ground.

'You're so clumsy. Can't you do anything right?' The riding teacher rolls his eyes. 'We'll just have to practise more. Your father won't be happy that you've not learned anything yet.'

'Don't tell him,' I beg the instructor. 'Papa pays for the lessons and never asks whether I'm making progress. It's part of my therapy.'

'But it's my duty to inform him. Your father wants me to report to him.'

'But then I'll have to go back to the clinic,' I say, my voice cracking. I shake the dust off my boots.

'You should have thought of that before, Lisa.' His face hardens. 'You have no grit, and your anxiety makes the animals nervous.'

He doesn't know I hate horses.

'Why don't you simply tell my mother that I have no talent for riding?' I try again. 'She's just over there.'

'That's enough. I'll tell your father you have no interest whatsoever in learning to ride – you simply refuse to learn. And then you will have to face the consequences.'

My riding whip is lying in the sand where I dropped it when I came off the horse. I pick it up and walk towards him. He's stroking the horse's nose and talking to it quietly. He can calm down horses, but not me.

'Please don't tell my father,' I whisper. 'I'm so afraid of him.'

'I have to take the horse back to the stable.' The trainer turns his back on me and walks off. I follow him, my head hanging down. From the bar I can hear Mama's loud laughter. As usual she's telling everyone about her career in the theatre. I hear glasses clinking. They're drinking a toast to her past successes.

'You're drinking yourself stupid,' Papa once said to her, before slamming the door shut on her and coming up to my room.

'What do I have to do to stop you telling Papa?' I step behind the riding teacher and begin unbuttoning my shirt.

'Stop that!' he growls. 'You're making things worse.' He takes his phone from his pocket. 'You can listen while I talk to your father.'

46

He turns around and starts dialling the number. I'm still holding the whip and, taking a deep breath, I swipe the phone out of his grasp.

'Are you insane?' He steps towards me, raising his hand. 'Enough is enough!'

Before he can say anything else, I strike him across the face with the whip. His skin bursts open and blood spurts out. He begins to yell. A stable hand comes running; he wrenches the whip from my hand. More and more people rush into the stable. The trainer holds his hands up in front of his bleeding face.

'I didn't mean to do it. It was the whip that did it,' I stammer. I lower my head and stare at the ground. No one must see my tears. 'It just happened.'

But nobody listens. They all surround the trainer. They pat his shoulder in sympathy and tend to his wounds.

'What has my naughty girl done this time?' My mother appears. Her eyes are as cold as her heart. 'I was just talking about my last big role and you interrupted it,' she accuses me angrily. 'You always mess everything up.'

She doesn't embrace me, but that's no surprise. She has never taken me in her arms. And how I long to be held by her, to feel protected. Particularly now, when everyone is turning against me. I am all alone here.

Then Papa's dark motor glides through the gates. It stops in front of the stables. Silently the window glides down.

'Get in,' he says quietly.

'Where are we going?'

'To the clinic.'

11

It was a mild evening as Olivia cycled to see her father. She was try-ing to focus on the traffic, but the phone call with Reiter was still troubling her. 'The case will be closed very soon.' It had sounded so definitive and felt like a slap in the face – everyone involved would now go back to their everyday life.

Me too, of course. Olivia only just managed to swerve away from a car whose driver had ignored the cycle lane. *We'll all just get on with our lives and forget that people like Jonathan even exist, because we like our peace and quiet. But he has rights too. He was my patient and we owe it to him to find out how he really died.*

She locked her bike to a basement metal fence at her father's block of flats and went up to the second floor, but then nearly fell over the rubbish strewn all around the hallway when she opened the door to the apartment.

'Papa, where are you? What's happened?' Olivia stepped over the squashed yoghurt pots, spilled milk and dried orange peel. 'What have you done?' Her father was sitting in his favourite arm-chair, humming. 'There's rubbish everywhere! And what's happened to you?'

Leopold was covered in milk, tomato juice and traces of chocolate.

'He wants to build an opera house for his mistress in the middle of the jungle,' Leopold said, pointing to the television, which was again showing the old Herzog film.

'Now listen to me, Papa,' Olivia began, planting herself in front of the TV set, but her father tried to look past her to the screen. He was giggling like a child.

'OK, watch the film, and I'll run you a bath in the meantime,' Olivia said, giving up the battle.

She was pouring bath oil into the water when Juli's voice suddenly echoed in her mind.

'Mummy, please use the pink bath oil. It smells of strawberries.'

'Of course, my sweetie.'

It had been the last bath with her daughter. Juli had sat in the warm water, blowing bubbles, and they'd both drunk Juli's favourite lemonade. At that moment life had never been more beautiful. Olivia had felt like taking the whole world into her happy embrace. Then she'd heard some clinking downstairs.

'Michael, is everything OK?'

'Yes, I just dropped a glass from the tray. Have a lovely time, my princesses.'

'Did you get out the pink frilly dress for me from the wardrobe?' *Juli asked, clapping her hands with joy.*

In that moment Olivia would never, never have dreamed that in one turn her life would change from pink to black.

'Olivia, is my bath ready? I'm filthy. Can I watch telly in the bathroom?'

'You always watch the same film,' Olivia said as she dried her hands.

Leopold came into the bathroom, and Olivia noticed that his eyes were clear and piercing. He took his dirty jumper off and smoothed his hair with both hands.

'Can I ask you something?' Olivia had to hurry, because Leopold's lucid moments never lasted long. 'Last time you told me that you knew Lisa Manz and that she was a difficult girl.'

'Now she is a dead girl,' her father added. 'She died a few years ago. Why are you asking me? Why are you interested in her?'

'One of my patients found her rucksack and a day later allegedly committed suicide. He gave me this piece of jewellery. Have you ever seen it before?' Olivia held up the pendant for Leopold.

'Yes, it could be the pendant from Lisa's necklace. She thought the snakes would bring her luck, but they didn't prove so lucky for her at the clinic.'

'How do you know?'

'I worked in the acute wing too. Have you forgotten? She was often taken there when there was trouble at home.'

'Did she run away from home? What happened there?'

'She was a typical borderline case, although she did once attack my colleague Nils like a wildcat. She could be quite fierce, but then again she was a frightened girl in need of help.'

'Nils? Do you mean the Nils who works at our clinic?'

'Yes, Nils Wagner – he's the head now. Lisa was his patient too. I only worked with her occasionally, after she had another breakdown and was aggressive towards everyone.'

'Her files must still be at the clinic,' Olivia said.

'Of course. Nils often videoed her as well. It was a kind of experiment he'd devised.'

'What kind of experiment?'

'Nils wanted to analyse Lisa's behaviour. Sometimes he videoed her for over twenty-four hours without allowing her any sleep.'

'Unbelievable. Was that legal?'

'It was a scientific experiment to make her better. I don't know any more about it.' Leopold shrugged his shoulders. 'You'll have to ask Nils the details. It was his idea and his patient.'

'Do you know where the files and the tapes are?'

'After Lisa's death it was probably taken to the secret archive.'

'A secret archive?'

'Yes, it's in the basement. That's where they store the patients' files that shouldn't be made public.'

'I've never heard anything about it.'

'It's director-level information,' Leopold said and smiled mischievously. 'But I still have a key to the archive – forgot to hand it in. I bet the files are in there.' He giggled again like a small child.

'And where is that key?' Olivia asked.

But Leopold didn't respond, no matter how much Olivia probed.

'What was going on in Lisa's head? What did you talk about in therapy?'

'Lisa? Who's Lisa?' Suddenly her father was looking at her without comprehension again. His shoulders had dropped, and he appeared years older.

'We just had a conversation about Lisa Manz.'

'Don't know her. I didn't have an affair with her either. Why are you always so jealous, Flora? You know I only love you.'

'Papa! Pull yourself together. Focus on the present.' Olivia grabbed her father's arm and shook him gently. She wanted to know more about Lisa. She didn't want him to sink back into his forgetfulness. 'Papa, concentrate! When did Lisa disappear from the clinic? How was that possible at all? Please tell me!'

'I want to have a bath with Flora now. Flora loves the water. She grew up by the sea, you know.'

'I don't want to hear it any more.' Olivia clapped her hands over her ears. 'Please stop with your stories about Flora. I want to know more about Lisa.'

'The illness comes in phases. On some days, the patient is completely normal.'

'Are you talking about Lisa? Was she ill? Did she have schizophrenic episodes?' Olivia asked hopefully. Maybe she'd be able to tease more information out of Leopold.

'Who is Lisa?'

'OK, Papa.' Olivia dropped her hands in resignation. It was no good. Her father had sunk back deeper and deeper into his old memories. In a clear moment, though, he had talked about a secret archive in the basement of the clinic. Who else could she ask about it? Was this secret room another figment of her father's imagination? No, Leopold had been absolutely clear when he'd mentioned it. Olivia helped her father into the bath and gently soaped his back. Afterwards she helped him put on his pyjamas and then tucked him into bed, as if he were a small child. When she was sure he was fast asleep, she quickly cleared up all the debris lying around the flat into the bin and then quietly left. Downstairs on the street, she got her mobile out and looked for a piece of paper with a number. When she finally found it, she knew what she had to do.

12

The men were sitting in a gourmet restaurant in the luxurious Golden Quarter in Vienna's city centre.

'An ex-inspector came to see Richard Manz today,' Nils Wagner, head of the psychiatric clinic, said to the man opposite. Nils had invited him for lunch after his old friend Richard Manz had called him. After five years of silence on this gruesome case, suddenly things were moving again, and it could easily develop into something serious. Whatever it was, it had to be stopped.

'An ex-inspector? Can only have been Levi Kant,' Kurt Mayer said. He was chief of the Vienna police. 'What did he want?'

'He had photos of a rucksack belonging to the dead girl,' Nils said. 'Theresa freaked out and I had to inject her with a sedative.' He took another forkful of steak tartare from his plate. 'How come you don't know about it?'

'I don't interfere with the day-to-day actions of the force. If I knew the details of every single case I'd end up in your clinic myself,' Mayer said. He called the waiter and pointed at the half-empty wine bottle and his glass. 'Fill it up,' he commanded.

'But it's not an everyday case,' Nils retorted. 'It's about Lisa Manz. Her parents are beside themselves. After five years, all the old wounds are being ripped open. You must put a stop to it immediately. Why is this old copper still meddling with things? Wasn't he sidelined years ago?'

'I'll have a chat with his former boss. Lisa Manz's murder was the only case Kant couldn't solve – that's why he's interested in the new developments. It's understandable.' Mayer took another sip of wine. 'Anyway, the case has been solved now, so I've been told.'

'Please see to it as soon as possible. I'm not interested in the motives of a washed-up copper. Sort him out!' Nils insisted. He looked at Mayer. You didn't have to be a psychiatrist to recognise that Mayer was completely unfit for the post of chief of police. He was an armchair policeman who happened to be a member of the right party. Luckily, he was a weak character who could be easily influenced.

'But we've found the perpetrator. Inspector Reiter is already writing up his final report, before it goes over to the prosecution service.' Mayer smiled uncertainly. 'As you can see, everything is quite under control.'

'Reiter won't be causing any difficulties?' Nils asked. He was not happy with Mayer's answer.

'How do you mean?'

'Well, what if Reiter's not sure it was a suicide and mentions it in his report?'

'Maybe I should take a closer look.' The chief of police nodded and rubbed his hands nervously.

'Yes, maybe you'd better. And what about Olivia Hofmann, the psychiatrist?'

'I think Reiter has recorded her statement, but I don't know if he'll include it in his report.' Mayer shrugged his shoulders.

'Listen to me, Kurt,' Nils said, bending forward across the table, 'just see to it that everything goes smoothly.' Leaning back again, he noticed his tie had caught some specks of steak tartare. 'Thanks to you, I've now ruined my tie,' he growled.

'OK, first thing tomorrow morning I'll ask for Reiter's report.' Mayer topped up his glass again. 'There's no need to worry, Nils. Everything is fine. It was a cold case, and now it's a closed case.' He patted Nils's hand, but the other man winced as if he'd been touched by a poisonous snake.

'A murder case is never closed,' he said.

13

Levi was at home, sitting at his desk and looking out through the window at the Vienna night. For decades now, he'd lived in Leopoldstadt in the Second District. It was the same area in which his grandmother, Esther, had lived; her old flat was only a few streets away. Levi passed the building every time he went to the launderette. And every time he passed, he stopped to read the names on the Stolpersteine – the brass plaques set in the pavement, bearing the names of the people who'd once lived there. Rosa, Rahel, Rebecca and Nathan, children of the Rosenzweigs. They'd been his grandmother's friends, until they were taken by the Gestapo in the middle of the night, together with their parents in March 1938. At first it was said that they'd left the country, but after the war the terrible truth came out. They'd been deported to the concentration camp in Dachau where they'd suffered an awful death. Levi's grandmother only survived the deportation of her own family because she'd been in the cellar getting coal. From then on, she'd never dared to go back to her flat and remained in hiding in the cellar. Until the end of the war she carried on living as an illegal, being hidden by friends and frequently moving around.

Levi never visited the synagogue, but had noticed with satisfaction that a strong Jewish community had again established itself in the quarter. On his windowsill stood a menorah, the Jewish seven-branched candlestick, one of the few signs of the religion into which he had been born. On the floor next to him was the pile of student essays. He'd taken his work home so he'd not be late in returning them. From the room next door, he could hear Rebecca playing the piano. The notes hung in the night air like shimmering pearls.

His mother had also played the piano. Levi's thoughts drifted back to his childhood and he pictured himself as he'd been then – a little boy shyly entering his grandmother's living room with his head down. It was always dark in there, the gloomy atmosphere of the room made even more so by the many dusty volumes of Jewish history. Just as gloomy and dusty as the memories that so often haunted his grandmother.

He remembered one time when he'd tiptoed quietly through the room to the window where Esther, wrapped in a coat that was much too big for her petite frame, always sat in her rocking chair, staring out. It seemed at first as if she hadn't noticed him, although of course she had. She never missed anything that was going on.

'Sit next to me, my boy,' Esther said without looking at him.

'Why are you always looking out of the window, *Omi*?' Levi asked, kneeling next to the old woman's chair.

'I'm on watch,' Esther replied. 'Always on watch.'

'Are you afraid of something?'

'Not now. Because now I know the people who terrorise others. If you know where the danger comes from, you don't have to be afraid any more.'

'And what do you see out there?' Levi asked quietly. He'd got up and looked out of the window. The street was dark, with only a few cars parked at the kerb and an old man walking his dog. Levi squinted. 'I don't see any dangers,' he said.

'You don't see the danger, but then suddenly it's there. That's why I'm always on watch. When the men turn the corner over there, I will have to disappear, I will have to go to the cellar, because they're coming to round us up. And every time I think about it, I begin to feel very cold.' Esther wrapped the coat tightly around her frail body.

'Is that why you're always wearing this coat?' Levi asked.

'No. The coat contains my memories. They were given to me so they didn't get lost.'

'What memories?' little Levi asked. He didn't know what she meant.

'Memories are thoughts, words or things that take us back to former times,' Esther said. Only now did she turn to Levi and stroke his head. 'You will remember me later in life when you see this coat.'

She sighed and lifted herself from the rocking chair, propping herself up on the windowsill with both hands. The coat hung heavily around her, seeming to weigh her down.

'My memories are very heavy,' she said and unbuttoned the coat. 'None of the people who gave them to me ever returned.'

Carefully she opened the coat. The lining looked like a patchwork rug, a colourful landscape of lives. Right at the top a moth-eaten teddy bear stared out with its shining glass eyes.

'Every patch is a pocket,' Esther continued. 'And every pocket contains a personal treasure of a member of our community which I was asked to keep safe. I call it "the Coat of the Unforgotten".'

'It sounds like a fairy-tale,' Levi said. 'Can you tell me the story, please?'

14

It all began when my mother, your great-grandmother, sent me to the cellar to get coal. As it was very cold, I put on her coat. It was the end of March 1938, shortly after Hitler had annexed Austria. That was when the really bad times began for us. All the true Nazis now dared to come out of their holes, and the persecution of the Jews began.

While I was shovelling the coal into the big scuttle, I heard a noise and peeked out of one of the narrow windows near the ceiling, through which I could just about see the pavement outside. A dark car had stopped in front of our house. Several men got out and banged at the front door.

'Open up! Police!' they shouted.

'Gestapo!'

I froze in front of the coal heap and held my breath.

'Do the Goldmans live here?' they barked at the caretaker woman who had reluctantly opened the door.

'Yes, second floor,' the woman answered timidly.

'Get out of the way!'

The men stormed past her and stomped upstairs. I tiptoed up the cellar steps and into the hall.

'What are you doing here, Esther?' All of a sudden, the caretaker stood in front of me, both hands to her cheeks. 'The Gestapo are at your parents' flat!'

'Why? What have they done?' I asked, because I could not imagine that my parents would have done anything wrong.

'Because they're Jews. Like you,' she said. Then she grabbed me by the neck and pushed me back towards the steps to the cellar. 'Hide, otherwise they will take you as well,' she whispered urgently.

I wanted to say something, but then I heard my mother's voice upstairs. 'My daughter isn't here. She's abroad.'

'Where exactly?' a man asked.

'In Switzerland. Skiing.'

'So you can afford a skiing holiday, you filthy Jews!'

'The Austrian state awarded it as a prize for an excellent pupil,' my mother countered.

Then I heard a loud slap and knew that the man had hit her. I can hear her cry out to this day.

'Don't lie to us, Jew woman. That's rubbish!' It was the voice of Egon, who used to own a small shop nearby. He'd had to close his business because of the economic downturn and since then worked as a casual labourer, but now his time had come. 'It's cold and you don't even have your stove lit. Maybe your brat has gone to get coal. Where is the cellar?'

My heart stopped. In panic I ran back, climbed onto the coal heap, slid down the other side and with both hands dug a hole to hide in alongside the wooden partition. I hastily pulled some coal over me and closed my eyes. Then I heard the steps. Heavy, intimidating, grim.

'Search the coal heaps.'

Egon's voice echoed and multiplied in the low-ceilinged cellar, turning into a choir of horror.

'It's too dirty here. Nobody there. Maybe that Jewish slut didn't lie for once, and the brat really is abroad.' The voice was that of a younger man, and I knew this one too. He was a good-looking young fellow with blond hair whom my father, the doctor, had treated for free several times. And this was how he demonstrated his thanks for the care my *father had shown to everyone in our quarter. So many people we knew had become our enemies.*

'Maybe you're right,' Egon agreed, and I heard the men stomping up the steps again. Then there were loud bangs outside. Later I realised this was the sound of the men throwing all my father's books, his medical equipment and papers out of the window and onto the street.

A short time later I heard the car starting, and they drove off. I stayed behind with the ghost-like silence towering over me like a dark wall. Much later I crawled out from under the coals and wrapped Mama's coat tightly around me. I still didn't dare go upstairs but sat down on the rough cellar floor, frozen.

When I looked out of the window again, I saw the heaps of books and all our other things, sodden by the rain, soon to disappear to a dump somewhere.

Then I saw Mister George, my teddy bear, lying out in the dirt. Without thinking I ran up the stairs, past the startled caretaker, out into the street and grabbed hold of him shortly before he was swept into the gully by the rain.

'There you are, my little one,' I said, pressing the sodden, dirty bear to my chest.

'Come back immediately,' the caretaker hissed. 'Nobody must see you!'

The woman grabbed my arm, pulled me into the hall and pushed me towards the cellar steps.

'Don't you dare come out again,' she whispered, threatening me with a raised forefinger. 'You'll get me into serious trouble.'

'I'll never do it again. Promise.'

When I was back by the coal heap, I stroked Mister George's wet fur, just like my mama stroked my hair that last time. I wanted to push the teddy into one of my coat pockets, but he was too big.

'I can't leave you out here,' I said to the bear. His button eyes stared back at me.

During the night, by the dim glow of the street lamp shining through the window, I crept through the other cellar rooms and eventually found some useful scraps of material. All I needed now was a needle and thread, but where to find it? I sneaked upstairs and scratched at the caretaker's door like a cat.

'You again?' she whispered after she'd pulled the door ajar. 'What do you want?' Anxiously she looked around the hall. 'You can't stay here.'

'I don't want to. I only need a needle and some thread,' I said and raised my hands imploringly. 'Please.'

'What for?' The caretaker shook her head and considered it for a second. 'OK, but then you have to disappear downstairs again.'

A short time later she opened the door and gave me what I'd asked for.

'There you are. Tomorrow I'll bring you something to eat. To the cupboard under the stairs where nobody can see it. That is all I can do for you.'

'It's more than enough,' I whispered and wanted to take her hand to thank her, but she hastily pulled it back and slammed the door shut.

Down in my cellar I crept on top of the coal heap under the narrow window leading out to the street. In the light of the street lamp I began to sew a pocket for Mister George into the lining of the coat, using the scraps of material I'd found. It took me the whole night, but by the time it was getting light again, it was finished. My teddy's button eyes were shining when I stuffed him into the pocket. Now at least he had a home.

I was exhausted, so I hid behind a wooden crate, wrapped the coat tightly around me and fell asleep.

I was woken by something softly touching me. I startled. Was it a rat? But then I saw the dirty face of a boy, somewhat younger than me, maybe eight years old.

'I saw you yesterday in the street. I followed you,' he stammered.

'What do you want?' I asked him, my heart in my throat.

'You saved that teddy bear. Where is it?' the boy asked as he looked around.

'I've made him a home,' I said and opened my coat. Mister George's head was sticking out of his pocket. His eyes shone in the dim light.

'What a lovely home,' the boy said, sounding like an adult. He turned and clambered over the coal heap, and I heard his quick steps running up the cellar stairs.

'What's your name?' I called after him in hushed tones.

'Aaron,' the boy said. 'See you again.'

'See you again.' The words rang through my head when I was alone again in my hideaway. Would Aaron report me to the police? When all was quiet, I crept upstairs and hid in the small cupboard under the stairs. The caretaker had kept her word, and I found a crust of hard bread and a mug of milk. I lapped some of the milk like a cat and then dunked the bread in to soften it, but I couldn't stay up there for too long, because the other tenants would soon be back from work, and among them were a few hardcore Nazis who would love to report a stray Jew.

The rest of the day I sat behind my coal heap, feeling very sad. How I missed my parents. In those dark hours I imagined being all alone in the world, dying a lonely death and being forgotten forever.

'Hello, I'm back.' Aaron's face popped up, startling me.

'I didn't hear you coming,' I whispered.

'I can sneak like a Red Indian,' Aaron declared proudly.

'You have to go. It's not safe here,' I said, looking over the coal heap towards the steps.

'I know, but there's something I'd like you to look after for me.' Aaron opened his hand and showed me a piece of silver jewellery.

'It's a pendant,' I said and looked at the boy. 'Where did you get it?'

'From my mother. I've told her about you. She thinks you should hide it until these bad times are over, so we don't get forgotten.'

'What's so special about it?' I asked.

'It's not your usual piece of jewellery. It's a locket. You can look inside.' Aaron opened the ornament. Inside was a tiny photo of his family: grandparents, father, mother and children. Aaron was among them.

'Why are you giving it to me? What am I supposed to do with it?' I asked in surprise.

'The locket was blessed by our chief rabbi, Israel Taglicht. No bad people must ever get hold of it. You have to keep it safe for our family, so we don't get forgotten. Put it into one of the pockets inside your coat. Like you've done with your teddy bear.'

'I'll have to sew a pocket for it first,' I said. It was true what Aaron said. If they rounded him up with his family, the locket would be the only evidence they ever existed. This family should not be allowed to be forgotten.

In the night I cowered again under the small window and sewed the next pocket into the lining of my coat. This one was smaller and made of a piece of red velvet, which I'd found on the floor in one of the empty cellar rooms.

'Psst! Can you keep this, so it doesn't get lost?'

I shot up from my half sleep and in a panic ducked out of my coal heap.

'Don't worry, Esther. It's me, Rahel Rosenzweig.'

A young woman was kneeling in front of me, the yellow star of David stitched to her worn jacket. With trembling hands, she held out a small booklet, wrapped in blue paper.

'It's my diary. I don't want the Gestapo to get it.'

'Why me?' I asked Rahel.

'Aaron told me about you. That you have many wonderful pockets in your coat where you keep things so we don't get forgotten. Please, would you do that for me as well?' She was holding the book towards me in desperation.

'Yes, I'll keep it for you.'

Then came the night again and I felt my way through the abandoned cellar rooms looking for scraps of fabric. In a corner I found a musty tablecloth, one part of it still intact. It was brocade, and my fingers soon started to bleed as I had to press the needle through, time and again. That too took me until the morning, but then the new pocket for Rahel's diary was finished.

The following days and weeks went very quickly. More and more people came to me in my coal cellar, asking me to keep their beloved items from being forgotten. Now they also brought me needles, thread and pieces of material, even a beautiful ornate thimble. Soon the legend of 'the Coat of the Unforgotten' had spread all over the district, and I became worried that the story of the magic coat would also be picked up by the Gestapo.

'And what happened next?' Levi asked, his cheeks burning with excitement. 'Are all the things still inside this coat?'

'No, I donated them to the Jewish Museum Vienna,' Esther said, her eyes welling up.

'But why?' Levi asked quietly.

'Because none of the owners ever came back.'

15

The memories of his grandmother faded away, and Levi sighed and looked at the cabinet behind him in his office. He hadn't opened it for five years, as he'd made a solemn promise to Rebecca. But the situation had changed, so Levi fished the key from the desk drawer and then, taking a deep breath, got up and opened the cabinet. He knew the contents very well, of course, but he still winced when he saw the photographs stuck to the inside of the door of a charred body, pictured from various angles. One showed a close-up of the blackened skull with the teeth, which had survived the fire, sticking out like those of a wild animal. Each image showed what was left of Lisa Manz after she'd been killed.

Levi's finger glided over the files on the shelves. Copies of the Lisa Manz case documents. He should be happy that the case now seemed to have been solved. Jonathan Stade was Lisa Manz's murderer, Reiter had told him. When Levi asked for evidence, Reiter had at first been reluctant but then became more open, for old times' sake. The chain of evidence was nearly complete. Jonathan Stade had been in the same clinic as Lisa Manz and had no alibi for the night that Lisa was burned to death. Stade had stated that he was sitting in the gardens of the clinic, but no one had seen him there. There had been an unknown car in the car park and Stade could easily have used it to drive to the scene of the murder in Burgenland and back. At the time that had not been enough to arrest him, but now they'd found Lisa's rucksack in Stade's flat and the handwritten confession. Levi would also have probably closed the case, if he'd still been in charge.

Somehow, he was just not able to let go of the files and photos. He'd thought of Lisa every day for five long years of his life – could it really be over at last? Lost in his reflections, Levi took out one of the files and turned the pages. It contained transcripts of the interviews of the suspects, and he knew them all by heart. He'd read them so often as he searched for contradictions.

His mobile rang. An unknown number.

'Hello?' he asked reluctantly.

'Olivia Hofmann here. Remember me?'

'Of course.' Levi pictured the attractive woman with the pale green eyes. 'What can I do for you?'

'There's a secret archive containing a videotape at the clinic where Lisa Manz last stayed. Did you know that?' Olivia came straight to the point.

'What clinic do you mean, and what are you talking about?'

'The clinic she disappeared from. I'm going there now to have a look. Do you want to come with me?'

'Do you know how late it is?' Levi asked. 'And, by the way, I have nothing to do with it any more. Plus, the Lisa Manz case is closed.' Levi leaned against the cabinet. *This psychiatrist is certainly stubborn*, he thought.

'I know. I've spoken to Inspector Reiter. But Jonathan Stade was not a murderer. Quite the opposite – he himself was murdered. Are you coming now or not?'

'Wait until tomorrow. Nobody will be around now who could help us.'

'OK. If you say so. Sorry for the late call.'

Before Levi could respond, Olivia hung up. Shaking his head, he looked down at his mobile and put it back in his pocket.

'You're not getting into that again, are you?'

Levi jumped at the sound of Rebecca's voice. Slowly he turned around and lifted both hands in defence.

'There's some news,' he apologised and was about to close the doors to the cabinet, but Rebecca prevented him.

'You have a serious problem, Levi Kant,' Rebecca said. 'How can you live year after year with this picture of someone who was burned to death?' She pointed to the photo of the charred skull. 'Do you dream of it? Do you smell the charred flesh? Do you get some kind of kick out of it?'

'I've not opened this cabinet for five years,' Levi said defensively. 'As I promised you.'

'But you constantly think about it,' Rebecca shot back. 'Did you deliberately seek out danger because you couldn't solve the case?' She indicated Levi's damaged leg.

'Don't be ridiculous.' Levi was overcome by a wave of exhaustion. He was tired of arguing with Rebecca about a case that was not even his any more. He told her what had happened.

'So your colleague has solved the case after all,' Rebecca said. Then she stepped closer to Levi and stroked his stubble with both hands. 'And now we can take this ugly cabinet and everything in it to the dump. Who rang, by the way?'

'Olivia Hofmann, a psychiatrist. She doesn't believe that the Manz case has been solved. And maybe she's right,' Levi added.

'I won't stand for it if you start meddling with that case again, Levi. Last time, the tension between us meant I couldn't even play the piano and I couldn't bear that to happen again.' She dropped her hands. 'You're a lecturer at the police academy. You promised me that our life from now on would be settled. If you start trying to dig up more dirt again, we'll both be very lonely.' Rebecca's dark eyes stared at him. 'Understood?'

'Please calm down,' he said. 'It's just that this psychiatrist is very persistent. It was one of her patients who killed himself. You have to understand.'

'Do I really have to ponder why a patient of a psychiatrist has killed himself?' Rebecca said, fiddling with a strand of her grey-streaked black hair.

'No, but I'm thinking about it,' Levi replied.

'And why? Is she more interesting than me?'

'No, certainly not. I promise you that by the end of this week the cabinet will be taken to the dump.' Levi gave Rebecca a kiss on the forehead. 'The music you were playing earlier was very beautiful. Who's the composer?'

'It was by Einaudi. I've often played it before, but you never listened.'

'From now on I will always listen,' Levi answered, pulling her closer, but she wriggled out of his grasp.

'First this horrible cabinet has to disappear from our lives,' she said. 'Only then will Lisa Manz no longer stand between us.'

16

It was a moonlit night when Olivia arrived at the imposing building that housed the clinic. It was housed in a restored palace that a relative of the Stonborough-Wittgenstein family had donated to the Psychiatric Association between the wars.

Walking across the car park, Olivia could see there was a light on still in the acute wing. She wanted to avoid running into anyone, so waited until the night nurse on reception disappeared into the small staffroom to make herself a cup of coffee. Quickly she went in through the front door and crept along the walls to avoid the surveillance cameras. Reaching the heavy iron basement door, she opened it carefully and sneaked down the steps. The light at the bottom of the stairs was dim and all she could tell was that she was standing in a broad corridor. She pulled her mobile from her rucksack and turned on the torch to light her way.

The long corridor was crammed with discarded hospital beds, walking aids and wheelchairs. Mattresses leaned against the walls next to tall metal drip stands that reminded her of the gallows. Numerous iron doors on the right-hand side mostly stood open. Many of the rooms contained stacks of old furniture and were unlikely to serve as an archive.

The left-hand side of the corridor was taken up by the pathology department, where they carried out the post-mortems on patients who had died at the clinic. That left only two rooms at the end of the corridor. Both doors were locked. Olivia knew from her father that the rooms in the basement were interconnected so that in an emergency you could run from one to the next.

She walked quickly back to the path lab. The small emergency lamps gave barely any light, but she could see that most of the gleaming steel tables were empty, apart from two. These tables stood side by side and each contained a body covered with a green sheet. As she passed them, she noticed a pale arm sticking out from under the sheet. The skin on the inner arm bore numerous fine cuts and scratches from pieces of glass or razor blades. Carefully Olivia peered under the covering.

She saw the smooth face of a girl who had been in therapy with Nils. Her young face looked relaxed, as if she was sleeping. Olivia had to swallow hard. She knew about the circumstances of this case; everybody at the clinic had been talking about it. They'd found the girl dead in her bed. In her anxiety she'd swallowed a spoon and choked. *We're here to help our patients, to show them the way back to the light. But for many the black tunnel ahead is too long, and the light is drowned in darkness*, Olivia thought. Gently she pulled the sheet back over the girl's face.

Holding up her torch, she noticed a screen standing against the far wall and moved it back to discover an inconspicuous sliding door leading into the next room. As expected, it was locked. Carefully Olivia took out the keys she'd found in her father's sugar bowl. She tried one after the other, becoming impatient when none of them worked. Offering up a small prayer, she tried the final key. It fitted, and she slid the door open, sighing with relief.

The beam of light glided over the walls of the secret archive. The high shelves contained hundreds of files in large cardboard

71

boxes. She checked shelf after shelf by the light of her torch. Each cardboard box was labelled with a date and the name of the patient, each one documenting the tragic fate of a disturbed soul.

But there was nothing for the relevant year, nor under the name she was looking for. She did, however, find a photo of herself, her father and Nils, who at the time had been the clinic's assistant director. Presumably it had fallen out of one of the boxes. Instinctively Olivia put it in her rucksack. By the time she'd searched through most of the aisles of files, she was covered in dust, but hadn't found anything about Lisa Manz. Disappointed she sat down on the floor to think.

Suddenly there were voices in the path lab, and the light flickered on. Two nurses quickly approached.

'Someone's forgotten to close that door over there,' one of them said.

Olivia held her breath, looking around the room in panic. There was no way she could hide between the aisles. Then she saw a set of shelves not quite tight to the wall, and quickly pressed herself into the gap. Her elbow nudged a box and it slid off the shelf before crashing to the floor.

'What was that?' It was a different voice.

'Probably a mouse or a rat,' her colleague said.

'I'd better check everything's OK in there.'

Olivia made herself as flat as possible, trying to squeeze herself further in behind the shelves. There was a dry click, and suddenly the archive was bathed in a harsh neon light.

'Hello?' the man called.

There was a rustling under a shelf, and a tiny mouse shot across Olivia's trainer.

'Mice in here,' the man informed his colleague. 'We'll have to report it.'

'Come back. What's in there has nothing to do with us – it's for the medics only. Just help me get these two bodies back to the morgue,' the other one said.

Olivia's heart was racing with relief as the two nurses disappeared. Slowly she slid from the gap back into the aisle and sat down, then collected the files that had spilled out of the box as it fell.

A name jumped out at her from the front of a file: Lisa Manz. Quickly she opened the folder and found notes about Lisa's stay at the clinic. She'd been in therapy with several different doctors to start with, but then only with one: Nils Wagner. The notes ended in the middle of a session, as if the following pages had been taken out. Quickly Olivia shoved the folder into her rucksack and got up.

She crept through the path lab and up the stairs. Just as she was scurrying across the empty foyer, the doors of the lift opened and a man in a white coat came out. He was looking at some notes on a clipboard so didn't notice her at first, but then he raised his head and smiled.

'Doctor Hofmann, what are you doing here at this time of night?' It was Simon Berger, a junior doctor, who was probably on nightshift. Many thoughts whirled through Olivia's head as she pretended she hadn't heard him.

'Doctor Hofmann, you surely haven't been seeing a patient at this late hour?' Simon repeated his question.

'No, I was looking for something,' Olivia said and took the rucksack from her shoulder. She opened it and pulled out the photo she'd found.

'My father wanted to see this photo. He's lost in his memories,' she said, holding it up for Simon's inspection.

'Sorry, I had to ask as I'm responsible for the whole ward tonight.'

'I understand.' Olivia smiled and put the photo back.

'I'm sorry about your father, by the way,' Simon said.

'Thank you.' Of course, everyone at the clinic knew about her father's illness.

Simon took a step towards her and looked at her with curiosity. 'You're all dusty, Doctor Hofmann!'

'Oh dear. I cleaned my father's flat earlier, that's why. It was then that he remembered this photo. He wanted it straight away.'

'Well, patients can sometimes be like dictators,' Simon said. His pager beeped, and he shrugged his shoulders.

'Have to go. There's a crisis on the secure ward. Maybe we can talk more another time,' he said and ran off through the foyer.

Narrow escape, Olivia thought once she was back on her bike. She could hardly wait to go through Lisa Manz's file.

17

LISA'S DIARY

The red rucksack is the only thing I have left. I bought it from a nice-looking boy in a vintage shop. Mama hates second-hand things and wanted to throw it out, but I wouldn't let her.

'Peace and quiet at last,' she sighs, pressing her script to her chest. She's no good at learning her lines any more, but I can't tell her that. 'You're going back to the clinic,' she says. 'It's better for you and better for us.'

'Papa wants it?' I say, and wish she'd take me in her arms, but instead Mama turns her back on me and steps in front of the large mirror.

'Come here, my baby,' she says suddenly, looking at herself in the mirror. 'Don't we look like sisters?' I go and stand next to her. 'Two beautiful blonde fairies,' she sighs theatrically.

'I don't want a sister but a mother who will help me. Do you know what happened to me when I went to the clinic last time?'

'I don't want to hear anything about it.' Mama puts her hands over her ears and takes a step back.

'Oh, Mama, why can't I stay with you?' I'm struggling to hold back my tears.

'That's not possible. When I was fourteen, I was nothing like you.' Mama walks even further away from me. 'I always wanted to become an actress and be a star.'

'But then you married Papa, and you never had your career,' I say.

'You have no idea.' Mama sounds offended. 'And you have no right to criticise my life.'

'But you're unhappy – that's why you drink so much. Maybe your parents were happy together and cared for you,' I say. I'm getting upset. I can sense that I'll lose control again soon.

'But you have everything here.' Mama looks around our large family home. 'You have designer clothes, a horse and the most expensive mountain bike money can buy. Despite all of this you're obnoxious and ungrateful.'

'I want a family.' My voice is shaking now. 'I don't give a shit about money and all that stuff. This rucksack is the only thing that means anything to me.'

'Don't talk such rubbish. That disgusting rucksack is just like your head.' She taps her finger on her temple. 'Inside, everything is all filthy and confused.'

'Mama, I don't want to go to the clinic,' I whisper and begin to sob. I know that Mama hates tears, but I can't help myself.

'You attacked your riding instructor. That's not normal. You need treatment, Lisa.' She shakes her head in resignation. 'Apart from that, you know the doctor. He looks after you very well.'

'But I'm afraid of the clinic *because* I know the doctor.'

A car draws up outside and a short time later the doctor enters the front room. I turn to the wall, because I don't want to see him.

'You've been very naughty, Lisa,' I hear him say behind me. 'A young lady of breeding doesn't attack her riding instructor.' How I hate this man's ingratiating voice. He really is the big bad wolf.

76

'Good of you to come. We're at the end of our tether with her,' Mama says. 'Lisa's things are in that awful rucksack.' She leaves the room without even blowing me a kiss.

'Mama?' I call after her, but quietly.

She doesn't turn around. For her, I am already gone.

In the car the doctor looks at me. 'You're in the best place with me, Lisa. Believe me.' He puts his hand on my thigh. 'If you behave yourself, you can soon leave the clinic again.'

Slowly his hand slides higher up my thigh. His fingers are icy, and a cold shudder goes right through me. I don't want this to start again but I stay still, because I know that everything will be much worse if I resist him.

'I'm so happy that you're coming back with me,' the doctor whispers, nearly inaudibly. He turns the car on the gravel drive. I can still open the door and run off, but where would I go? I have nobody. I'm all alone.

'We'll have a good time together,' the doctor whispers.

I turn around desperately and look out of the back window. For a fleeting moment I think I see Mama waving to me from the bay window but it's only Lucrezia, the Filipina maid, who now wipes her tears away with her apron. She's the only person in this world who loves me. The house disappears very quickly and by the time we reach the gate it's just a speck in the distance. I'm numb all over. I'm unbelievably sad. I want to die.

18

The next morning Levi Kant sat in the office of his former boss, Helmut Klein. Klein had had him picked up and brought to head-quarters as soon as Levi's last lecture was over. Levi had a vague idea what this might be about, so he waited in silence for the man to speak.

'Thank you for taking the time,' Klein said, rubbing his hands as if he was cold.

'I always have time for you,' Levi answered.

Klein smiled awkwardly and placed his folded hands on the desk. 'How is teaching going at the academy? I hear the students are mad about you. I always thought you were a born teacher.'

'I like my work but you've not asked me here for small talk.'

'You're right,' Klein said. 'Reiter was being a good colleague when he kept you informed about the Lisa Manz case.'

'Yes, it was very kind of him,' Levi said. 'After all, it was me who led the investigation at the time.'

'Then you will certainly be very pleased that we can now finally close the case. The rucksack has been identified conclusively as belonging to her. We also found a photo of Lisa Manz in Jonathan's flat, taken by him five years ago. The fingerprints on the rucksack have also been identified as belonging to Stade. And then there's the handwritten confession.'

'Have the experts confirmed that it is in Jonathan's handwriting?' Levi asked.

'Well, it was written in capital letters so it can't be confirmed one hundred per cent, but it doesn't matter so much – it's only a small link in the chain of evidence.' Klein folded his hands behind his head and rocked on his office chair. 'Another cold case solved,' he said with relief, leaning forward again to adjust the silver photo frame on his desk. Levi knew the picture showed Klein's two daughters.

'The perpetrator has killed himself to avoid his rightful punishment. That's regrettable, but also good for the taxpayer.'

'Is that what you asked me here for?' Levi said. 'Reiter could have told me all that over the phone.'

'There is one more thing,' Klein continued. 'The chief of police rang me. You visited the Manz family?'

'Yes, I wanted to inform them that the rucksack had been found.'

'Richard Manz has complained to Mayer about this.'

'Why?'

'His emotionally vulnerable wife had a breakdown and you are held responsible.'

'I rather think he caused that himself.'

'Now listen.' Levi sensed that Klein was finding it difficult to hide his anger. His ex-boss rocked forward in his chair, his face darkening. 'By pretending to be an inspector and harassing people, you've gone too far. If I don't speak up for you, you'll soon be in serious trouble.'

'Has this got anything to do with the suicide? Because I have my doubts about him being Lisa's murderer?'

'There are no doubts,' Klein insisted, leaning back with a heavy sigh. 'My God, Levi, can't you finally forget this case?'

'Doctor Olivia Hofmann, the psychiatrist, also has her doubts about Stade's suicide. She thinks he was pushed because she saw a shadow behind him at the window.'

'And you believe that?' Now his superior sounded as if he was talking to a little child.

'Doctor Hofmann's statement seemed very credible to me. What does Reiter reckon to it?'

'Reiter thinks it's purely a matter of self-preservation. This Doctor Hofmann is, after all, partly responsible for the death of her patient.'

'She doesn't appear to be displaying any guilt,' Levi countered.

'Is she good-looking?' Klein asked abruptly.

'What? Yes, she's attractive. Why do you ask?' Levi gave Klein a puzzled look and then, with some irritation, ran his fingers through his greying hair.

'Because she's obviously left an impression on you. A shadow, indeed. What nonsense!' Klein muttered, scrunching a ball of paper to throw into the wastepaper basket. 'As far as we're concerned, the case is closed and will go to the prosecution service.'

Following the conversation with his former boss, Levi went back to his office in the police academy where he had a long conversation with two students who were applying for a bursary to the FBI academy in Quantico and needed his advice. When he saw the extensive application forms they had to fill in, he couldn't help but admire their enthusiasm and persistence. After they left, his thoughts went back to Lisa Manz. Why couldn't he let it go? Why did he have such a bad gut feeling about it all?

Lost in contemplation, he was startled when his mobile rang.

'I went to the clinic last night,' Olivia said immediately, not bothering with any preliminaries. 'There really is a secret archive, like my father said.'

'Did you find anything on Lisa Manz?' Levi asked, straightening up in his chair. Olivia Hofmann's energy was contagious.

'Yes, I took her file home with me.'

'Isn't that against the rules?' Levi said. And then he asked, 'And did you find anything interesting? Do we have any evidence?' The urgency in his tone was clear.

'You just said *we*.' Olivia's voice sounded quite cheerful now. 'Yes, there are notes about a twenty-four-hour experiment, but I need to take a closer look.'

'Maybe it'll throw some light on the case.'

'Does that mean you and I are now trying to get to the bottom of these murders together?'

'What do you mean, murders?'

'We're dealing with two murders here – or do you really believe that Jonathan Stade killed himself?'

'If it wasn't suicide, it was a very cleverly executed murder,' Levi conceded.

All of a sudden, he felt years younger. This was his chance. An opportunity to give his life meaning again. His goal was to find justice – justice for Lisa Manz, justice for Jonathan Stade.

'I'm due to give another lecture in a while. Can we meet tomorrow morning in Café Stein, close to your office? We can go through the file and develop a strategy.'

'Thank you. You really are one cool guy,' Olivia said happily.

Levi's face broke into a smile. When was the last time Rebecca had called him a cool guy?

19

Olivia was pushing her bike across the car park when she heard a voice behind her.

'So was your father happy with the photo?' Simon Berger, the junior doctor, asked.

'Photo? What photo?' Olivia turned to give Simon a puzzled look.

'The one with you, your father and Nils Wagner. The one you so urgently needed to pick up at the clinic last night?' Simon tried to jog her memory.

'Oh, that one. Yes, very much. He was very happy about it.' Olivia gave him a fake smile, parked the bike and walked quickly towards the entrance. She was still excited after the phone conversation with Levi. The case was starting to move. With a professional by her side the dark secrets around the two dead people would soon be revealed.

'I admire you,' Simon said, struggling to keep up. 'You have your private practice, work two days a week here at the clinic and you look after your sick father. That is truly admirable.'

'Nothing special about it. I like my work. I can help people who don't find life very easy and are marginalised in our society.' Olivia waved to the nurse on reception – a different one from last night. While she was waiting for the lift, she continued, 'Looking after my father is only natural. I can't desert him. He didn't desert me when I was having a bad time.'

They entered the lift together, both looking straight ahead, their figures multiplied to infinity in the mirrors all around them. Olivia noticed that Simon was watching her shyly. She in turn risked a quick glance at him. He was tall and slim with dark, curly hair and wore dark-framed glasses that made him look serious. Somehow he was also quite attractive. If she remembered correctly, Simon was about thirty years old, nearly ten years younger than her. Suddenly she felt herself blushing. What was she thinking? Had the conversation with Levi excited her so much that she was projecting her enthusiasm in other directions? Well, whatever. She wasn't an old woman yet.

But then she thought of Michael and Juli and her good mood drained away. No, she wasn't in the slightest bit interested in a relationship. She didn't want another man in her life. She was still trying to rebuild it from the fragments their departure had left behind. Levi, however, was different. Levi was an ex-policeman she was working with on a case. Levi was no more than a colleague. No, men had no place in her life any more.

Then suddenly their eyes met in the mirror, and both smiled involuntarily.

'Are you seeing your father again tonight?' Simon asked.

'Why?' Olivia said.

'Well, they're showing an interesting film at the Studio Cinema. I thought you might like . . .' He didn't finish the sentence.

'I don't know yet,' Olivia said, avoiding a clear answer. No, she didn't want to change her life, but then again, what was so wrong with going to see a film? It would distract her from her thoughts.

'What time?'

'I'll send you a text. Give me your number.'

'OK. See you later.'

The lift doors opened, and Olivia straightened her shoulders as she walked swiftly down the corridor. She could feel Simon's eyes following her, but she didn't turn around.

She sat down at her desk in the small office and put her head in her hands. Maybe it was time to begin to live normally again. She'd have to discuss this in her next supervision session with Ulf. He'd put her on the right track.

After staring into space for a while, she switched on the computer and searched the clinic's intranet for more information about Lisa Manz. The new patient log had only been installed two years ago, however, so her search was in vain.

Olivia had little time for further investigation for the rest of the morning. The clinic was very busy, as always on the days around the full moon. Her last patient before lunch was an unemployed man who'd had a breakdown in a supermarket and smashed up the shelves. He'd appeared confused and the police had brought him here. To calm him down, the doctor on duty had given him a sedative. Now he was sitting numbly on a chair in one of the treatment rooms with a beautiful view of the park-like gardens of the clinic.

'Your name is Kaspar Trauner and until a year ago you were employed by the Agruna Company. Why were you dismissed? You'd worked there for two years in middle management.' Olivia looked up from the file and waited for a response.

'I wasn't dismissed. I quit the job,' Trauner said. 'I wanted to do something different.'

'But the file from the unemployment bureau says that you were dismissed, otherwise you wouldn't have been entitled to benefits straight away.'

'That's wrong. I wanted to realise my potential for once in my life. It's that simple,' Trauner said, his voice shrill.

'OK, OK. It's not important.' Olivia removed her glasses and put them on the desk. 'I can offer you confidential counselling. Not here, but in my private practice.'

'I can't afford that.' Trauner shook his head and flicked an imaginary speck of dust off his grey suit. Olivia observed him closely. The man was in his late fifties, clean-shaven, well groomed and wearing a suit and tie. *He's trying with all his might to keep up the appearance of being a successful manager.* The thin red veins around his nose and the watery eyes, however, told her that the man might have a considerable alcohol problem.

'Social services will pay for ten sessions, then we'll see. It's up to you.' Olivia turned to her computer and opened her diary. 'What about next Tuesday at eleven o'clock?'

'I'll check to see if I can fit it in,' Trauner said and took a diary, seemingly unused, from the inside pocket of his jacket.

'Have you seen the people waiting outside?' Olivia asked. 'They all want counselling. Please tell me if you want the appointment or not. Otherwise I'll give the session to someone else who might be more in need of it than you.'

'We're in luck. I have it booked as a day off.' Trauner got up and offered Olivia his hand. 'Looking forward to working with you.' He shook her hand as if he'd just been offered a job.

Olivia watched him walk to the door, then went over to the window. On a park bench, a man and woman were sitting together, then a little blonde girl ran towards them and was embraced by both. Watching the scene, Olivia swallowed hard. It could be her and her family down there. She took a deep breath and quickly left the office.

The cafeteria was in the old stables of the palace and when she entered, she noticed Simon sitting at one of the tables by the back wall, leafing through a psychology magazine. She didn't want to talk to him so went straight to the counter. Waiting in the queue, she saw Nils Wagner enter. He was involved in a conversation, his mobile to his ear and didn't notice her.

It's now or never, she thought, taking a deep breath.

20

Nils Wagner felt relieved as he sent off his report to the board of the clinic. Nothing could possibly happen now.

He was just leaving for the cafeteria downstairs when there was a knock at the door.

'Can I talk to you for a moment, Doctor Wagner?' It was one of the nursing assistants who now nervously averted his eyes. 'It won't take long.'

'What is it?' Nils asked, but didn't offer the man a chair.

'I was on night duty yesterday,' the nursing assistant began slowly, 'and I had to take two bodies to the morgue with a colleague.'

'Please get to the point. I don't have much time.' Nils began to drum his fingers on the desk in irritation.

'The door to the archive in the cellar was open. That's never happened before.'

'The door to our archive was open?' Nils repeated. 'But only doctors and directors have access.'

'I know. We didn't want to go in, but then we heard sounds inside, and I went to check. There was an open cardboard box on the floor. In Aisle M. It struck me as very suspicious.'

'In what way?' Nils asked, feeling his hands getting sweaty. Who on earth could be looking for something in the archive in the middle of the night? What could be so important that it couldn't wait until the morning? 'What else struck you as suspicious?'

'The open box had the letter M on it as well.'

'M, you say.' Nils frowned. It might not mean anything, but he couldn't afford to get careless now, just as everything was falling into place. 'Anything else?'

'My shift was nearly over and my wife was waiting for me in the car park. We both had a cigarette before we got in the car. It's too unhealthy, smoking in the car.'

'Get to the point,' Nils said sharply.

'Someone ran quickly across the car park.'

'Did you recognise the person?' Nils asked, folding his arms.

'It was Doctor Hofmann.'

'Are you sure? There are no lights in the car park.'

'Absolutely. She got on her old bike. I'd recognise that bike anywhere.' The assistant nurse broke off and cleared his throat. 'You'd ordered us to tell you whenever we saw something unusual. Doctor Hofmann was not on duty that day, I know that. I know the rota by heart.'

'Well done, good man.' Nils got up and patted the man on the shoulder in a patronising manner. 'How is your wife, by the way? Have you been on holiday recently?'

'Well, we can't afford it this year,' the assistant nurse said sheepishly. 'My wife's ordered so much stuff online and unfortunately we can't return it.'

'Well, that's bad,' Nils said. 'Maybe our legal department can do something about it, Herr . . .' He glanced quickly at the nurse's name badge. 'Herr Goranowitsch.'

'Really? That would be ever so generous, Doctor Wagner.' He was visibly moved and pressed Nils's hand.

'Well, I can't promise but I'll do what I can.'

When the nurse opened the door to leave, Nils called after him, 'This has to stay between you and me. Not a word to anyone or I can't help you.'

Nils waited a few minutes, then left his office as well. On the gravel path to the stables he took out his phone and dialled a number.

'There might be a problem. Somebody has been sniffing around our archive.'

The answer he got didn't reassure him.

'Don't worry. I informed the board of the clinic today.'

He opened the door to the cafeteria and ended the call. Out of the corner of his eye he spotted Olivia Hofmann in the queue by the buffet counter.

How awful to have to stand in a queue with all these other people, he thought and forcefully pushed his way to the front.

21

Balancing her full tray, Olivia headed towards Nils Wagner's table. He was checking his emails on his phone.

'Do you mind if I sit down?' Olivia didn't wait for an answer and took a chair. 'I'd like some information from you.'

'Olivia, how lovely to see you.' Nils smiled, beckoning for her to join him. Then he leaned back and ran his hands through his thick grey hair. It was a bit too long, as usual. 'To what do I owe this honour?' he asked. Then casually he placed his mobile on the table so Olivia could see the photo of an attractive woman he'd just received. 'I always get this kind of photo,' he said and then switched the phone off. 'You have no idea how keen women get when they hear that I'm the head of the clinic,' he continued, leaning forward conspiratorially.

When Olivia didn't respond, he straightened and looked her up and down openly. 'You're looking good,' he said.

Olivia thought she detected a condescending or ironic tone in his voice. Why did she always get the impression that Nils had an ulterior motive or meant the exact opposite of what he said?

'Considering how you looked only a few years ago,' Nils added with a smile.

Olivia didn't want to think about that. When her whole life collapsed, she hadn't been able to look after herself for a while.

She'd always been the one to cook the meals for her small family, but after they disappeared, she couldn't be bothered and started to live on fast food. As a result, she'd piled on the weight and had become increasingly unhappy with her body. She'd compounded the problem when she'd started to turn to sweets for comfort. It was a vicious circle. Olivia lost all confidence and gave up on her social life. Soon all her friends had vanished, and she stayed hidden in her flat most of the time. Even her work at the clinic no longer gave her any satisfaction.

When she learned about her father's illness, however, she'd realised that she had to take control. She changed her eating habits and went into therapy herself, more for her father's sake than anything else. She couldn't bear how quickly he was deteriorating in front of her eyes.

To be able to afford the increasing costs for his care and medication, she also took over his private practice. Her life changed from senseless vegetating to meaningful work, and within a short time Olivia had lost weight and discovered a new passion: cycling.

Nearly every day, in the early morning, she cycled through the empty streets of Vienna. She relished the cold air on her skin and the opportunity to think without being disturbed or distracted. It also had the added bonus of burning a lot of calories.

'Do you still run the Missing Persons Group?' Nils said, interrupting her thoughts.

'Yes, but we're on a summer break,' Olivia replied curtly. She didn't want to talk about it with Nils. The Missing Persons Group was a meeting place for men and women whose nearest relatives had disappeared. While listening to the others' stories, Olivia could also explore her own feelings.

'Oh yes, I forgot. I've had rather a lot on my plate in the last few weeks and haven't been at the clinic much, but then you know that, don't you?' Again Nils leaned forward and whispered, as if he was telling her a secret, 'I've been put forward for a job in government.'

'How exciting. What kind of job?' Olivia pretended to be curious. The man's vanity was excruciating, but at least she knew exactly how to deal with someone like him.

'It's a ministerial post – but that is strictly between you and me.'

'Of course.'

'I don't know whether to accept it, with so many crazy people around.' Once again he ran his fingers through his hair in a studied manner. 'Actually, what is it you wanted to know?' he said abruptly, looking suddenly serious.

'Do you remember a girl named Lisa Manz?' Olivia asked, observing him closely for his reaction.

He stirred his coffee, looking bored. 'No, who is she?'

'She was a patient with us when she was fourteen. She disappeared from the clinic five years ago. A short time later she was found murdered.' Her father might have got it all wrong about Nils being her doctor, but it was confirmed in the secret file.

'Oh, that terrible story, yes. Poor girl. I do remember now.' Nils looked at her, clear regret in his eyes. 'Why are you interested in her?'

'You were working at the clinic at the time, as head of the acute wing.'

'Yes, that was my department.'

'My father mentioned that you were trying out some new therapy methods five years ago.'

'Yes, we wanted to advance with the therapies we were offering and were testing out the theories of "Free Psychiatry" on our patients,' Nils answered reluctantly.

'And what exactly did that involve?'

'I can't tell you that – it's confidential. You should know that.'

'My father mentioned that you kept Lisa awake for twenty-four hours while filming her. Surely that's against the law.'

'Ah, all the stuff your father comes up with, but that's only to be expected with his illness.'

'Don't be mistaken, my father often has moments of clarity. And in any case, there are notes covering Lisa's treatment from that period.'

'How do you know?' Nils asked quickly.

'I just know, that's all,' Olivia replied. She'd probably made a mistake in mentioning the notes but it was too late now.

'How come after all these years you're suddenly interested in Lisa Manz?' Nils asked, looking at her sharply.

'One of my patients found Lisa's rucksack in a derelict house. A short while later he was dead.'

'Ah, so that's what this is all about. You're referring to your patient Jonathan Stade who committed suicide. I understand.' Again, Nils made a face that attempted to show something like sympathy.

'How do you know?' Olivia was surprised. 'None of the papers have mentioned his name.'

'The police informed us.'

'Why would the police inform the clinic?'

'Not the clinic, but the board of directors. I'm the chairman. I took the post over from your father – you're surely aware of that.'

'Of course.'

'Well, this is a good moment to talk about it, Olivia.' Nils lowered his voice and once more looked around furtively. 'The rules say I'll have to order an inquiry. You'll have to give a statement to the board. Stade was your patient, after all.'

'But I had nothing to do with his death. Jonathan only wanted to give me Lisa's rucksack – that was the reason I went to see him.'

'You were in his flat and didn't prevent your patient's suicide.' Nils shook his head as though he couldn't believe it. 'Olivia, maybe you have too much on your plate. I mean . . . your private clients, your work here at the clinic, your father who needs care, and I don't even want to mention what happened five years ago. I think this is all getting a bit much for you.'

'I wasn't in his flat, but downstairs out on the pavement. By the way, it has not been cleared up yet whether it was a suicide.'

'The police have given us very definite information.' Nils raised his eyebrows arrogantly.

'What exactly happened to Lisa at the time?' Olivia said, probing again. Nils's supercilious manner was beginning to get to her. 'Nobody noticed when she disappeared from the clinic. That's more than a little unusual, isn't it?'

'That's enough now, Olivia.' Nils scrunched his paper napkin into a ball and threw it on the table. 'You should consider your next steps very carefully. Forget Lisa Manz and mind your own business. It would be a shame if we couldn't supply you with those expensive drugs for your father's Alzheimer's any more.'

22

The black diary with the golden clasp was wrapped in a white plastic bag.

'Someone anonymous sent me pages from Lisa's diary.' Out of breath, Olivia held the packet towards Levi, who had just opened the door to his flat. She was soaked through. It was pouring outside – one of those short but heavy summer showers. Raindrops fell from her short dark hair leaving dark spots on her grey T-shirt dress.

'I wrapped it up so it wouldn't get soaked,' she said, opening the bag. The cover of the diary looked scratched and worn and not in any way like the diary of a typical fourteen-year-old.

'Come in, Doctor Hofmann,' Levi said, opening the door. 'I'll fetch you a towel – don't want you to catch cold.'

'Thank you, that is nice of you. Do call me Olivia. We are sort of colleagues now, after all.'

'Thank you, that would be much more straightforward. So how do you know it's Lisa's diary, and why are you bringing it now? I thought we were meeting tomorrow?'

'Oh, because her name's on the first page. I thought if I read it on my own, it would only upset me even more. I've had such an awful day.' Olivia told Levi about the unpleasant conversation she'd had with Nils Wagner and of his veiled threats.

'If we can prove that Jonathan Stade was murdered you have nothing to fear,' Levi reassured her.

'I'm a little more optimistic now,' Olivia replied. 'There are only a few pages in the diary, but they may offer a few more clues.'

'It's not the whole diary? Are you sure?'

'Of course I am. See how most of the pages have been ripped out?' Olivia said, opening the book.

'Where did you get it?' Levi asked.

'It was in my letterbox when I came home from work,' Olivia replied.

'There must be a sender's address then,' Levi said, thinking hard. 'Only the postman can access the boxes.'

'The lock on my box is broken so anyone can put things in. There was no sender's address on the envelope.'

'Where's the envelope? Have you only brought the diary?' Levi asked.

'I threw it away. It was a simple brown envelope,' Olivia replied, shrugging her shoulders.

'You really have no idea how the police work, Olivia.' Levi shook his head, annoyed. 'There could have been fingerprints on it. Who knows your private address, by the way?'

'Well, the clinic does, along with my colleagues and some of my patients in case of emergency,' Olivia answered sheepishly. 'Sorry about the envelope but it might still be in the wastepaper bin in the hall. I'll check as soon as I get home. Could we maybe sit down somewhere to go through the pages in peace and quiet?'

'I've not got much time. My wife will be home soon,' Levi replied.

'Is she the jealous type?'

'Yes, of this thing here.' Levi pointed to the filing cabinet in the living room. 'We rowed about it only recently – I had to promise to throw it out, along with all the Lisa Manz files. That's why it's better you leave before she returns home. It would cause another massive argument.'

'Of course, that's fine,' Olivia conceded, but from her expression Levi knew she couldn't really grasp why he wasn't allowed to investigate the case privately. But then, he didn't get it either.

'What does your wife do?' Olivia asked, taking off her wet sandals.

'She's a piano teacher,' Levi replied. 'She used to be a concert pianist but gave it up because she didn't think she was good enough. One of her pupils is performing in a concert tonight.'

'A wonderful profession, though it also sounds rather melancholy from the way you describe it,' Olivia said, wiping her face with the towel Levi had brought.

'Sometimes it's not easy,' Levi said. 'We're constantly working on Rebecca's low self-esteem – she's up and down the whole time. Anyway, why am I telling you all this? We're supposed to be discussing Lisa Manz here, not my marriage.'

'OK, OK.' Olivia pointed to a framed photo on the shelves. 'Is that you?'

'Yep. It was taken at my bar mitzvah. I was thirteen. That day I became a full member of our congregation.'

'You're an orthodox Jew?' Olivia was surprised.

'No, but I belong to the faith. I owe that to my grandmother, Esther.'

'What happened to her?'

'She only escaped deportation to Dachau by sheer luck. Between 1938 and 1945 she stayed in hiding, otherwise she too would have been murdered by the Nazis. Her only possession was a coat with many pockets in which she kept her things, along with mementos of many of her neighbours who were taken. She had a terrible time, but she never lost her sense of humour or her positive attitude. She wore that worn coat every time she went to the synagogue on Saturdays, right up until the day she died. I still have it. It reminds me to stay modest and content with my life. Not to complain about things, even when it feels like you're walking through a long, dark tunnel. Some people have had darker times than me, others less so.'

Olivia said quietly, 'Can I see the coat some day?'

'Sure, I'll show it to you at some point but for now, enough of the old stories.'

Levi waited until Olivia had dried herself a little more, then went to open up the filing cabinet.

'Wow, are these files all on the Lisa Manz case?' Olivia had stepped behind Levi. 'And that's where she was found?' She pointed to one of the photos of the crime scene.

'That's right. You can probably understand now why I was so determined to find the murderer. Only someone with a heart of ice and an implacable will could burn a young girl to death.' Levi clenched his fist and pointed to the photo of the charred skull with his knuckles. 'Whoever did this needs to be punished,' he whispered.

'Don't worry, we'll find Lisa's murderer,' Olivia said to comfort him.

'Either that or her murderer will find us . . .'

23

LISA'S DIARY

I'm sitting in one of the usual treatment rooms again. My heart is pounding. This morning they put me on an intravenous drip and my whole body feels numb. My face is reflected in the polished surface of the metal cabinets. It looks like a skull with long blonde feathers. My eyes are huge. I'm not Lisa any more.

'Take your things off,' the doctor says.

I don't have the energy to disobey. The white gown falls off my shoulders. I hate my body – it is so thin and scraggy, but when I eat, I put on weight, and I really don't want to be fat. Only cutting helps.

'You're quite a pretty young woman really,' the doctor says appreciatively.

'I don't like myself.'

'Have you been cutting again?'

'Yes, I do it often.'

The doctor takes one of my arms and looks at the scars. He clicks his tongue contemptuously. The arm is covered with new scabs and scars. When I look at myself in the mirror the cuts look an actual pattern.

'Why do you do that?'

'The pain makes me feel alive. I need to feel myself. I don't mind the pain.'

I hear the words, but I barely comprehend them. It's as though someone else is speaking through me.

'You have a sophisticated way of talking,' the doctor says. 'Are you intelligent, would you say?'

'I learned all this from my mother's scripts. I've been reading since I was five.'

'Do you like your mother?'

'Yes, I love her, but she hates me.'

'Why do you think that?'

'She says I destroyed her career as an actor and that whenever I'm away, she has her peace and quiet back.'

'And without the pain you feel like you're dead?' The doctor changed the subject. 'Would you like to die?'

'Maybe, but before that I'd like to leave my mark in this world.'

'What kind of a mark?'

'No idea.'

'Why did you attack the riding instructor?'

'Because he wanted to complain about me to my father.'

'Does your father control you?'

'He likes everything to be in order. For him, I'm just chaos.'

'Do you hate order and discipline?'

'When my father comes in my room, I have to control myself.'

'What does he want of you?'

'I'm not allowed to talk about it.'

'OK, let's leave that until later.' The doctor clears his throat. 'Your priority is to learn to accept your body and your feelings, then you will automatically stop the cutting. Stand up, please. We'll start the treatment now.'

I get up obediently and stand naked in front of the doctor.

'What's going to happen now?'

'You will learn more about your feelings.'

24

The sad passages from Lisa's diary were still echoing in Olivia's mind.

'It's outrageous,' she whispered, 'how much this young girl had to suffer!'

'To me it sounds like a clear case of abuse,' Levi said. 'She stands naked in front of a doctor – that alone is a scandal. Do you have any idea who that doctor could have been?'

'Nils is an arsehole, but I can't imagine he'd do something like that.'

'Who else could it be apart from Nils Wagner?'

'No idea.'

'Have you noticed that the diary is mainly written in the form of dialogue?' Levi asked.

'Yes, she's probably imitating her mother's scripts – to me it shows how much she wanted to please her mother, though it seems her mother always ignored her.'

'Do you think her father abused her as well?'

'It's possible, but he may also have carried out some coercive control.'

'In any case, her relationship with her parents wasn't good,' Levi said. 'There was no one she could turn to. I feel very sorry for her.'

'It happens quite frequently with children of rich parents. If the kids don't adapt, they're packed off to boarding school or a clinic.'

Levi looked at his watch. 'Rebecca will be home soon, so you'd better go now. Shall we still meet tomorrow?'

'Yes, as arranged.' Olivia felt she was being pushed out. She'd have loved to analyse the few pages of Lisa's diary with Levi all night, but now she felt rejected. She took the book from him and put it back in her bag. 'I'll take it with me. Maybe I can find out which doctor she's talking about.'

Soon afterwards, Olivia was standing back out on the pavement, unlocking her bike. The rain had ceased at last. She needed some distraction because Lisa's story would not leave her, and she didn't want to spend the rest of the evening ruminating on how Lisa's young life had gone so catastrophically wrong. Her mobile beeped to notify her of a text:

Cinema at eight o'clock. Are you coming?

Followed by a smiley face. It was from Simon Berger.

Olivia immediately sent back a thumbs-up emoji and pedalled off fast. She didn't have much time to get to the cinema.

'How lovely you could come,' Simon said, greeting her with a peck on the cheek.

'What kind of film is it?' Olivia asked after studying the poster. A man was carrying a beautiful woman without legs on his back towards the sea.

'It's a drama,' Simon answered, his voice low as if it wasn't right to discuss a serious film at full volume. 'The woman's legs were ripped off by a killer whale, but she's not giving up.'

'Sounds very positive.'

'Yes, it's inspirational,' Simon said, nodding. 'Maybe we could show the film to our patients as a kind of motivational incentive.'

'I'm not sure about that.' Olivia thought of her father endlessly watching his film. No, that sort of passive behaviour would not be right for her patients.

After the cinema they headed to a Schanigarten, one of the typical Viennese garden pubs. At first they talked about the film, which Olivia had liked. The acting had impressed her, but gradually their talk moved on from general topics to more personal ones.

'Do you cycle in all weathers?' Simon asked.

'Yes, it keeps me fit and gives me energy for the day and it strengthens my immune system.'

'Sounds like a great write-up for cycling.'

'Exactly!' Olivia laughed and took another sip of wine. The alcohol was relaxing her, and thoughts of Lisa had been pushed to the back of her mind. When was the last time she'd laughed so freely? She couldn't remember.

'I have a mountain bike. Maybe we could go on a bike trip at the weekend,' Simon said.

'I don't have a mountain bike, only a very uncool retro number.'

'But the way you ride, it looks very cool.'

'Oh, stop it.' Olivia waved him away. 'Nobody has ever described me as cool.'

'That's because you probably dazzle everyone with your good looks.'

'Oh yeah, probably.' Olivia smiled ironically and ran her fingers through her short hair. She hoped it wouldn't go grey as early as her mother's had done. Olivia didn't mind getting older, but she didn't want grey hair. Especially when she was out for the evening with a much younger man.

'I'll find an easy route for us. It shouldn't be a problem with your bike.'

'Yes, OK.' Olivia was amused.

All of a sudden she thought again of Lisa Manz and quickly had another sip of wine, trying to banish her from her mind. 'Tell me about yourself. I don't know anything about you,' she asked Simon.

'Well, I'm really quite boring – happy childhood, no problems in school or at university. Everything according to plan.'

'And girlfriends?'

'Never had time for that,' Simon answered, averting his eyes. He waved at the waiter to order another two glasses of spritzer.

'I don't believe you,' Olivia said.

Simon looked away, embarrassed. 'You caught me out. I have to confess, I never missed out on anything in my younger years.'

'You were working at the clinic five years ago, weren't you?' Olivia asked. 'Do you remember a patient named Lisa Manz, by any chance? Did you ever happen to notice her writing in a diary?'

'I did my traineeship there. You mean the girl who was later found burned to death? No, I never met her.'

Silence. Olivia felt that there was nothing left to talk about so started hunting through her bag for her purse.

And then Simon asked, 'What actually was it that happened to your family?' And the whole relaxed evening that had wrapped itself around Olivia like a soft duvet was ripped away and the familiar icy chill once more flooded her mind like a cruel spring tide.

'What do you mean?'

'I've heard some rumours at the clinic. Is it true that your husband and daughter simply disappeared one day?'

Olivia moved away from Simon, hurt and angry. Suddenly the atmosphere felt charged, like before a storm.

'What happened? Do you want to talk about it?' Simon insisted.

'There's nothing to tell.' Olivia's voice was hard now, and all of a sudden she was stone-cold sober. 'Everything's fine,' she said, slapping a twenty euro note on the table. 'I just need to go now.'

'What's the matter?' Simon said, running after her, but Olivia had already left the Schanigarten. Frantically she undid the lock on her bike, nearly crying now.

'It's just that I'm interested in you,' Simon explained from behind her.

'Don't bother,' Olivia retorted. 'Stick to women your own age.'

'Can we meet again?' Simon asked.

'At some point maybe. I'm tired now and I want to go home.'

'Olivia, please wait!' Simon called after her, but she didn't turn around and instead jumped on her bike and pedalled off.

Cycling around town for a while helped to calm her a little. Questions about Michael and Juli still threw her completely sometimes. Would that ever end?

She was approaching the Ninth District by now, near her office, and rode along Währinger Strasse before stopping off at an alternative arts centre. It was a mild summer evening and the restaurant in the courtyard was still busy, but she managed to find a table to herself. Her thoughts turned back to Jonathan and Lisa, but she resisted the urge to pull the diary from her bag.

Pleasantly relaxed and tired after another glass of wine, Olivia set off again. Her father came into her mind as she cycled along the now empty streets; she hadn't visited him today, but it was too late now. She just hoped that the person who looked after him two evenings a week had set the DVD to play on an endless loop. She wondered whether her father knew about Lisa Manz's strange disappearance from the clinic. She couldn't imagine that he did. He'd always been a psychiatrist of the highest integrity, with a reputation for treating people marginalised by society with respect and care, whether out in the rainforest or back home, here in Vienna. No, her father definitely would not know anything about what had happened to Lisa.

All of a sudden, a huge four-wheel drive with bright headlights shot out of a side street at high speed and raced directly towards Olivia, clipping her bike and throwing her into the air. As she crashed down on the road, she was aware only of the sound of the car driving away before everything went black.

25

The next morning, Levi waited in front of Kaffeehaus Stein on the Schottenring and looked at his watch. Olivia was more than half an hour late. He paced the pavement nervously, repeatedly trying her mobile but each time it went straight to voicemail. Finally, tired of waiting, he went into the Kaffeehaus. An hour and four espressos later he still hadn't heard from Olivia, so he set off for the police academy, hoping that her father was all right. She'd seemed so eager to meet when they spoke last night that he could only assume something serious had happened to keep her away.

Only a handful of people were present in the main lecture hall of the police academy when Levi went to stand at the lectern. It was his last lecture before the summer holidays and most of his students had started their internships with various police departments. The few students still around were specialising in outdoor forensics and Levi would be talking about it for the next two hours. He checked his mobile numerous times while he was speaking and projecting photos of different crime scenes onto the big screen, but still no news from Olivia.

Afterwards he dialled the number of the clinic.

'Can I please speak to Frau Doctor Hofmann?'

'One moment, I'll put you through,' the friendly voice at the switchboard said. Levi felt disappointment spread through him. Had Olivia really forgotten their meeting?

'I'm sorry, Doctor Hofmann isn't answering.'

'Is she not in today?' Levi asked.

'Oh yes, she was due in at two o'clock this afternoon. Wait, I'll try to find her on a different number.' He waited several minutes, then the voice of the receptionist came again: 'Strange, but nobody knows where she is.'

'Have you seen her at all today?'

'No.' The woman stopped to think. 'One moment, I'll just see if her bicycle's outside.' After a short time, she came back. 'No, her bike's not here either.'

'Thank you,' Levi said and ended the call. He tried ringing Olivia in her office but again he only got the answer machine. He was growing increasingly concerned and wasn't sure what to do, until he remembered a former colleague who might be able to help.

'Schmidt, it's Levi Kant here,' he said when the man answered. Schmidt ran the police radio system and Levi had once covered for him during an illegal surveillance. Schmidt owed him one.

'I need to track a mobile. ASAP, if possible.'

'No problem. What's the number?' Schmidt asked.

While they waited for the information to come through, Schmidt asked Levi how he was.

'Great. This lecturing job is just perfect for me,' Levi said.

'I never would have thought so. You loved your department heart and soul, didn't you?'

'Well, when the heart isn't in it any more, the soul doesn't have much fun either.' Levi was alluding to his injury. 'Have you got a signal?' he said, changing the subject.

'Yes, from near the hospital on the ring road. The mobile presumably is in the hospital there.'

'Thanks, mate. We're quits now,' Levi said to his ex-colleague, ending the call.

He quickly left the academy and jumped into his Saab 900. As usual, the four-lane ring road – the Gürtel – was one long traffic jam, and Levi mostly crawled along at a walking pace. By the time the dark double towers of the general hospital loomed into view, the journey had taken a full hour.

'Inspector Kant. I'm looking for Doctor Olivia Hofmann. I think she may have been admitted,' he said at reception.

'Doctor Hofmann, you said?' The receptionist scrolled through the lists on her screen. 'You don't know which department she might be in? We have nearly two thousand people here and thirty-nine clinical departments.'

'No, I'm sorry. Could she be on the patient register?'

'Sorry, our departments are not listed alongside the relevant names.' The woman shrugged apologetically.

'Would you please try the emergency department?' Levi suggested.

'The emergency department?'

'Yes, where you're taken after an accident.'

'You mean A & E.'

'Exactly.'

'Yes, we have an Olivia Hofmann. Bicycle accident, hit and run. She's in Room 237 in Wing B.'

'The same room number as in *The Shining*,' Levi said spontaneously.

'Where Jack Nicholson meets the beautiful stranger.' The receptionist smiled at Levi knowingly.

'Oh, another film buff,' Levi said, regretting that he didn't have time for a longer chat.

He rushed through the corridors towards Room 237. Looking through the glazed panel in the door, he saw a man with grey hair standing by Olivia's bed with his back to him. He wondered briefly whether to enter but decided against it and instead took the lift down to the cafeteria. He'd wait and see Olivia a little later.

26

When Olivia opened her eyes again, a blurred face that looked like Nils Wagner was bending over her.

'I told you it would end badly. With the state you're in, you just have too much on your plate at the moment,' Nils whispered, stroking her forehead gently. 'You're ruining your health.'

Olivia was too tired to respond. Her head was still swirling, and she closed her eyes. *It's only a bad dream*, she thought, but opening her eyes once more, she realised that Nils was no fantasy but an unpleasant reality.

'What did you mean when you said it would end badly for me?' she croaked.

'Everything will be fine, my dear. Don't worry. We'll see to everything.' Nils patted her hand patronisingly.

'What are you seeing to?' Olivia was breathing harder now. She had an appalling headache and wasn't certain that she'd understood Nils's words correctly.

'We'll look after you so you can get well again quickly.'

'What are you doing here anyway?'

'The police called me.'

'Why you?'

'They found your clinic ID card on you.'

'Ah, thank you.'

Olivia felt for the patient's file lying on the bedside table. Slowly the memory of last night and her accident came back. A car had driven into her and sped away. According to the file she had a concussion and some bruising. There must have been a guardian angel watching over her, she reflected.

'Can I have a look?' Nils took the file from her and read it closely.

'Oh, so there was alcohol in your blood.' Nils shook his head disapprovingly. He pointed to the sheet and then showed it to Olivia. 'What are you up to, Olivia? You were lucky.'

'I wasn't drunk, if that's what you mean. And it wasn't an accident. Someone tried to kill me.' Olivia tried to raise her voice, but her bruised ribs couldn't take it and her face contorted with pain.

'Calm down,' Nils said. 'Who on earth would want to kill you?'

'Someone who wants to prevent my investigations in the Lisa Manz case. Someone like you,' Olivia replied.

'Rubbish! You'd consumed alcohol and were nearly twice the legal limit.' Nils touched her arm reassuringly. 'I'll talk to the doctor and they'll give you a sedative, then they can give you a thorough check-up and perhaps we ought to look into referring you to a rehab centre.' He smiled confidently and adjusted his tie.

'Certainly not. I'm not ill. I'll be out of here tomorrow. I have to make money and can't afford to live on sick pay,' Olivia said.

'Take it easy, Olivia.' Nils's voice again sounded patronising. 'You can't work at the moment.'

'And why ever not?' Olivia tried to sit up, but it hurt too much. Exhausted, she sank back into the pillow.

'Well, apart from your normal difficulties, you now have an alcohol problem as well. Do I need to explain myself any further?'

'Oh, stop it. You know as well as I do that I'm not a drinker.' Olivia was shaking with anger. Of course she knew what would follow next. She felt utterly powerless.

'I'm sorry, but I can't change the facts. My advice is to go to the rehab centre in Kalksburg where you can undergo alcohol withdrawal therapy. In the meantime I'm going to have to suspend you from working at the clinic. It's for the best.' Again he patted Olivia's hand.

'Go away,' Olivia said, closing her eyes, 'and I don't want you coming back.'

'I can understand that.' Nils's voice sounded soft and superior. He was very sure of himself. Why was she so damn alone? Why was there nobody by her side who could help her in this threatening situation?

'One more thing, for your information.' Nils paused before he continued. 'Maybe it's not the right moment, but it's my duty to tell you.'

'What else?'

'The date for the inquiry by the board of directors is coming up soon. You will remember to attend, won't you?'

'Why are they carrying out this inquiry?'

'Do you really have to ask me that? A patient committed suicide in your presence. That's enough, isn't it?'

'It wasn't suicide. It was murder.'

'Not that again!' Nils shook his head, irritated. 'It was suicide. The police have confirmed it.' He looked at her pityingly. 'You leave me no choice.'

'You've organised this all very nicely,' Olivia whispered, closing her eyes again. 'You just don't want me to look into the Lisa Manz case – your patient, and your experiments with her.'

'Oh, Olivia, you and your fantasies! It probably runs in the family. Has your father told you anything else about Lisa Manz?'

'No, my father can't remember her. Can you please leave me in peace now?'

'Good, good. Well, look after yourself.' Nils went to the door, then stopped and looked back at her. 'Whether you believe it or not, I am on your side.'

'Whatever.'

Olivia turned her head to the window; the sky was blue, and the leaves were shimmering in the sunlight. The world outside was beautiful, and a stark contrast to the ominous grey thoughts swirling through her mind.

When she opened her eyes again, it was getting dark. A nurse had entered her room, followed by a doctor. The nurse changed the bag of saline, while the doctor asked, 'How are you feeling now?' He took a pen from his pocket and held it in front of Olivia's eyes. 'Follow the pen with your eyes,' he told her.

Olivia did as he asked, and he seemed happy with her response and tucked the pen away.

'Someone from the police urgently wants to talk to you. He's waiting outside. Are you happy to see him?'

'Yes, but talking is painful.'

'That's because of the bruised ribs. They'll take a while to heal.'

'Please send him in,' Olivia said.

The doctor went, leaving the door open, and then Levi was standing by her bed, looking down at her with concern. When Olivia tried a smile, his expression cleared slightly. He sat down on her bed and said, 'Thank God you're still alive, Olivia. Lisa and I need you.'

27

The door to Olivia's room opened gently and a nurse entered with a tray which she put on the bedside table. Levi got up and waited until the nurse had left.

'You must eat,' he said with concern. Olivia's face was bruised; there was a plaster on her left temple and she had dark shadows under her eyes.

'I'm not hungry,' she said.

'What exactly happened last night?' Levi sat down on a chair beside the bed. Olivia haltingly told him what she could remember.

'Sounds like you've been very lucky,' Levi said. 'I was getting really worried when I couldn't get hold of you.'

'You worried about me?'

'Yes, of course. And with good reason, it seems. I don't think this accident was coincidental. Who was the man who just visited you, by the way?'

'Nils Wagner, head of the clinic. Don't you know him from five years ago?'

'When Lisa disappeared from the clinic, we only questioned the doctor on duty. I meant to call in the other medics and nurses too, but never got around to it because of my accident. The case was taken over by a colleague.'

'So Nils was not on duty when Lisa disappeared?'

'No, but what did Wagner want from you now?'

'He's suspended me. He says I'm an alcoholic and should be sent to rehab,' Olivia said with a bitter laugh. 'What a mess.'

'You were drunk when the accident happened?'

'Of course not. If I'd really had that amount of alcohol in my blood, I wouldn't've been able to ride my bike. Either someone tampered with my blood test or there's been a mistake, but how can I prove it? It's like I've prodded a wasp's nest. Not only has a patient of mine died, but someone also wants to ruin my life.'

'Relax. If we can prove that Jonathan is not Lisa Manz's murderer, then his case will automatically be reopened and the questions concerning his alleged suicide will have to be asked again.'

'And how are we going to do that?' Olivia sounded hesitant, but Levi saw in her eyes that his words had given her some hope.

'What about the pages from the diary? Do you still have them with you?' he asked.

'They should be in my bag,' Olivia said. She tried to sit up, but Levi noticed how she grimaced with pain and carefully eased her back.

Olivia's grey dress was hanging in the wardrobe, filthy and with a long tear down one side. The bag was on the bottom shelf and Levi searched through it; if it really had been an attempt on Olivia's life, then it was also possible that the unknown enemy knew about the diary. But they were in luck.

'The diary's still here,' he said, holding it up triumphantly.

'We have to take it to the police.' Olivia was sitting up now. 'It's much too dangerous to keep it here.'

'No, we can't do that,' Levi said. 'Not a good idea.' He was thinking of the implied threats from his former boss. 'It would be far too risky.'

'For someone who's with the police, this is . . .?' Olivia raised an eyebrow.

'Five years ago, someone at the very top tried hard to interfere with my investigation. All further inquiries were stopped when I was in hospital and I couldn't do a thing about it.'

'Do you really think that someone was out to murder me?' Olivia asked in surprise.

'No, not to kill you, but to give you a warning. Now you're frightened, and that's exactly what they wanted to achieve. We really have to be extra careful now.'

'I'm not afraid,' Olivia said. 'I'm quite good in dangerous situations.'

'Don't underestimate your opponent's determination,' Levi warned. 'By the way, where's Lisa's file from the clinic, the one you borrowed from the archive?' He didn't want to say 'stole'.

'It's at my flat. I never got around to picking it up.'

'We need every bit of evidence we can lay our hands on. Every little detail can help. Every last piece of the puzzle about Lisa's final year is important.' He paused for thought. 'There has to be something somewhere that'll help unravel it all.'

'There is that gap of five days between Lisa's escape from the clinic and her death,' Olivia said. 'Maybe we'll find a clue as to where she was during that time and who helped her. That might put us on the trail of her murderer.'

28

LISA'S DIARY

I'm allowed to leave the clinic for the weekend. Papa has arranged it with the doctor – he wants to see if I've made any progress.

'You are aware of the shame you have brought on the family?' Papa says when I enter his study.

'I've done everything the doctor said.' I'm anxious and can barely stand still in front of Papa's desk.

'The doctor says that you're far from well enough to leave the clinic for good. Your emotional life is underdeveloped. That's why you're so aggressive.'

'But that's not true,' I say. 'I simply don't like his methods.'

'And what exactly is it you don't like?'

'Well . . . nothing . . .' I can't tell Papa what the doctor does with me. Papa would get very upset, and then everything will be my fault again. 'If I really, really try to be good at the clinic, will I be allowed home again?'

'We shall see what the doctor says.' Papa rises. 'Is your room tidy?' he suddenly asks. I feel the blood rising to my cheeks.

'Of course,' I stammer. My thoughts are racing. I left the window open so Ali could come in from the roof, but I've not been here for a while so hopefully he's found somewhere else to stay. It would be better if I checked for myself.

'I left my rucksack on the bed. I'll quickly put it away, then you can come.'

'No, we'll take a look right now.'

'There's really no need. Everything is shipshape.' I try to keep him at bay.

'That is really not for you to decide.' Papa grabs my arm in an iron grip and drags me out into the hall and up the stairs.

'Let go! You're hurting me!' I cry. It feels like he's dislocating my shoulder.

'What is all this noise?' Mama comes out of her room. 'Why are you shouting like that? I can't concentrate.' She stares at me disapprovingly.

'Papa is hurting me!'

'Nonsense!' Mama says, waving her script at me. 'Now get lost. I'm studying for my new role.'

My heart is pounding by the time he stops in front of my room.

'Open the door!' Papa commands and lets go of my arm. The room is tidy, the wardrobe closed. On my desk is nothing but the framed photo of Mama, Papa and me. I breathe a sigh of relief.

'And what is that?' Papa points to my bed. Ali is lying there, curled up and fast asleep.

'It's only a poor little homeless cat,' I say, stepping between the cat and my father, arms spread out wide.

'You actually let stray cats into our home? Have you completely taken leave of your senses? Cats breed uncontrollably and carry bacteria and disease. Like all animals. Have you not considered that I might have a cat allergy? Or your mother? Of course not. We have rules in this house, but you consistently break them.'

'Ali's only in my room,' I say, feeling my anger slowly overcoming my fear.

'So you've already named the animal? It's been here for a while then? You really are a very naughty girl,' Papa says with a sigh. 'Very well then, show me the cat and then we shall see.'

'Thank you!' I say and turn to the bed. Ali is purring and stretches as I pick him up. 'Isn't he cute?'

'He'll grow up into a big tomcat,' Papa says. 'Come on, give him to me.'

'You won't hurt him, will you?' I look at Papa doubtfully, but his face is inscrutable.

'No, he won't feel a thing. I am a doctor after all.' He leaves my room with the cat under his arm.

It's nearly midnight when I wake up. The moon is shining through the window and its cold rays fall as far as the door opposite. I get up quietly and step out into the corridor, then sneak along the gallery so I won't wake Papa. The stairs creak on my way down to the kitchen.

'Ali,' I whisper and put some milk into a bowl. Then I open the door to the kitchen garden and wait. Ali loves milk. I sit for hours on the cold step, waiting for my cat. I cry silently, feeling more alone than ever. Ali never comes.

Shivering, I make my way upstairs again. I stop in front of Mama's door, hesitate, then press the handle down. Mama sleeps on her back, wearing an eye mask. She's been suffering from insomnia for years now and there's a whole squad of homoeopathic remedies on her bedside table.

'Mama,' I whisper, 'can I come in bed with you?' I lift the duvet and slip in. Mama's body is thin and bony – she's always on some diet.

'I must be slim, or I won't get any roles as the young romantic lead,' she always says. But Mama hasn't had a lead role since she played Medea before I was born. Since then she's had to make do with bit parts. It's all my fault.

'Mama, can you hold me really tight?' I edge closer to her, but she pushes me away.

'You've woken me up now. You know how difficult it is for me to get to sleep,' she hisses. 'Get out of my bed this minute!'

'Mama, please let me stay! I promise I'll be quiet.' I'm begging her.

Mama sighs. 'Oh, for goodness' sake. Now I have a migraine as well, and it's entirely your fault. I can't cope with this. Thank God you'll be back at the clinic tomorrow and we'll all be able to get some peace again.'

It's no good. I go back to my room. The moon is still shining brightly and bathed in its silvery light I walk to the window as though on a luminous carpet. My room is on the second floor and I lean out of the window, looking down at the terrace below. Then I climb on the windowsill and sit there. My legs are dangling outside – and I spit. *If I jump now, I'll die.*

29

'That's just so sad,' Olivia said, gazing at Levi with tears in her eyes. He closed the diary and stroked his stubbly beard.

'For a fourteen-year-old, Lisa expresses herself very well.'

'She always wanted to become a writer,' Olivia said. 'It says that somewhere in her files, in one of the interviews they did at the clinic.'

'Any idea who this doctor might have been?' Levi asked.

'It was probably Nils Wagner.' Olivia looked questioningly at Levi. 'It would fit with all the things he's trying to do to me now.'

'But he'd hardly be so stupid as to make himself a suspect. I never once came across his name five years ago. Anyway, the place is only ever called the "clinic". Could she be referring to a different establishment?'

'Where else could it be?' Olivia asked. 'But you may be right, I suppose. The entries aren't dated so it could be older. It could have been written at any time.'

'Except that Lisa does mention that she's fourteen years old so it was during her last year in this world,' Levi said. He looked around. 'Can I borrow the key to your flat?'

'Why?' Olivia's hand went to her temple. She had a pounding headache and felt a sickness take hold of her.

'I want to get the files you found in the archive.'

'I'd rather do it myself,' Olivia said. She didn't want a stranger in her flat.

'But you're unwell,' Levi countered, 'and you need to stay in hospital.'

'I'm fine. I'll take a taxi to my flat, pick up the documents and come straight back.' Olivia could tell Levi was not convinced by her plan, and he was right – it probably wasn't a good idea for her to leave the hospital just yet. 'All right,' she conceded, 'here's the key. The file is in a brown envelope on the desk in my study, first door on the left – but promise me you won't go in my sitting room.'

'Why?' Levi asked.

'It's not very tidy.'

'I'm not bothered,' Levi said, 'but I promise.'

'I'll probably be much better tomorrow and can be discharged. In the meantime, you'd better take the diary. It won't be safe here. I can't even lock the wardrobe.'

'All right.' Levi put the diary in an inside pocket of his coat and rose awkwardly to his feet.

'What happened to your leg?' Olivia asked. She'd heard from Anna, her journalist friend, that Levi had been seriously injured in a shooting, but she wanted to hear more details.

Levi dodged the question. 'I'll tell you another time,' he said. 'You have your little secrets too.'

Olivia didn't respond, only looked at Levi thoughtfully. 'You're right. And those little secrets should remain little secrets.'

'That suits me just fine.' Levi raised a hand to say goodbye.

After he'd gone, Olivia stared at the clock on the wall. Levi hadn't insisted on finding out what had happened to her five years ago and she appreciated that. He was a sensitive person who respected her privacy.

The hands of the clock inched forward very slowly. Seconds became minutes. Minutes seemed like hours, and sometimes Olivia felt that time was standing still altogether.

She kept thinking of the car that had raced towards her. It was not some random accident. Her mobile beeped. *It must be Levi*, she thought, cheering up, but to her surprise it was her father's number on the display.

'Papa, what's the matter?'

'There . . . is . . . it is very untidy in my flat.'

On hearing her father's strained voice, Olivia started to panic, realising with a shock that she'd completely forgotten about Leopold yesterday and that his nurse had not been on evening duty either.

'Flora, there's a stranger in my flat,' her father whispered. 'He's messing everything up.'

'Who is with you, Papa? Papa, who is it?'

'You don't understand what I mean, Flora. I've kept everything. You always laughed about it, Flora, but it was meant to keep us safe.'

'Sorry, Papa, but it's Olivia here. What are you talking about?' Olivia was getting upset, and fear for her father was nearly choking her.

'You don't have to tell me anything. Stop rummaging around and then get out of my house!' The anger in her father's voice was quite clear over the phone.

'Stay calm, Papa, and do exactly what I say. Sit down on the sofa and switch on the telly. Do you understand me? You only have to press the red button.' There was an ominous silence at the other end. 'Papa, are you still there?'

Her father didn't answer, but Olivia could vaguely hear what was going on in the flat.

She had to do something and right this minute. Her father was the only person left in her family. He was her rock, and she just couldn't lose him as well.

With a loud moan Olivia got up. Once standing, she felt dizzy and had to cling to a chair for a moment before, very slowly and very upset, shuffling to the wardrobe to fetch her dress. Her face contorted with pain as she slipped it on and when she looked in the mirror, she was shocked at the dark shadows under her eyes and the deep wrinkles on either side of her mouth.

'Not a good idea to simply disappear from here,' she whispered to her mirror image.

But she had to go to her father. Gritting her teeth, she made it through to reception. The ward sister looked up in surprise when she saw Olivia.

'But Frau Doctor Hofmann, you can't just leave. You're injured and need to rest.'

'I'm OK. Please give me a discharge note to sign,' Olivia replied impatiently and raised a hand. 'And please call me a taxi.'

When the car arrived, Olivia had to hang on to the door because the pain was almost intolerable, but she couldn't give in – her father needed her.

30

Nils Wagner froze when he heard the croaky voice next door on the phone. Small beads of sweat formed on his forehead. For a moment he stopped searching the room and listened tensely to what the confused old man was saying. Coming from the other side of the wall, the words were scrambled and without meaning. Nils had entered the flat quietly through the narrow side entrance, formerly used by staff, which only had a very simple lock.

When the brain fails, even the most intelligent person turns into an idiot, Nils thought. He closed the door of the study quietly, so he'd not be surprised by Leopold Hofmann, his former boss, while rummaging through his flat. He hastily went through file after file, throwing them carelessly on the floor after he'd examined each one.

Olivia had told him that her father had not kept any files from his work at the clinic, but that was certainly a lie. Her eyes had given her away. You notice things like that as a psychiatrist.

After rummaging through every box without finding anything, Nils stopped for a moment. Leopold had been in this state for four years now. His decline had been surprisingly rapid, but in the past few months he'd become more stable, which was no doubt due to Olivia's loving care.

He could just ask Leopold directly whether he'd kept any files from his former work. Maybe he still had the documents relating to the experiments Nils had carried out at the clinic. If something like that became public knowledge, his planned political career would never happen. Maybe they'd even take away his licence as a psychiatrist. And what then?

Nils took a syringe from his pocket. Opening the door, he went out into the hallway. Leopold was now muttering to himself. Who had he been talking to? Probably to Olivia, but she was still in hospital so shouldn't present any danger. Nils wiped his forehead with his gloved hand then went through to the sitting room.

'Hello, Leopold,' Nils said with an evil smile. 'How are you?' He pronounced each word with care, so Leopold would understand him better.

'Who are you?' Leopold looked at him with suspicion. He didn't look well. His hair was unkempt, his shirt buttoned the wrong way and his trousers were stained. Quickly Nils walked towards him, rolled up the old man's shirt sleeve and jabbed the needle into his arm. It had an immediate effect. Leopold's pupils narrowed until they were only pin-size. The drug would intensify the dementia, but it also might have an impact on the long-term memory – which was just what Nils was after.

'I'm from the board of directors from the clinic,' Nils said. 'I need to ask you some questions.'

'Board of the clinic?' Leopold rolled his eyes and pondered the words. 'And what do you want to know?'

'I want to pick up the files you have here about your colleague Nils Wagner.'

'Nils? Ah yes, Nils the philanderer.' Leopold shook his head. 'Yes, I have a few things to say about Nils. His methods are not in line with our code of ethics. I've watched him closely and taken numerous notes about it.'

'Give me those notes. I'll pass them on to the board directly.' Nils stepped closer.

'You remind me of somebody.' Leopold winced.

'Sure, sure, we've met quite often at meetings.'

'If you say so,' Leopold said doubtfully.

'Well, where are the notes?' Nils glanced at his watch. Around ten minutes had passed since Leopold's phone call. Olivia might have asked someone to go and see her father, so he needed to hurry.

'I took notes over several years. Initially it was only rumours and there was no proof, but then I found a videotape concerning a patient called Lisa Manz and that was all the evidence I needed.'

'A videotape?' asked Nils, his pulse starting to race. 'Where is it?'

'I took a copy. All the files are in my study,' Leopold said. 'Let's go over there.'

He shuffled ahead of Nils to the hallway. Nils relaxed slightly. Soon all the incriminating material would be in his hands. Nobody could get at him any more. As soon as the effect of the drug waned, Leopold would forget all about their conversation and would sink back into his own little world.

'May I go ahead?' Leopold asked politely in front of the door to his study. With trembling hands, the old man pressed the door handle. 'Oh, what's happened here?' he asked, stopping in his tracks.

Damn, thought Nils. The files were all still on the floor, while a stack of torn papers lay on the desk.

'I guess the cleaning lady hasn't been,' he said in an effort to reassure Leopold. 'She'll be here soon to tidy everything up.'

'Ah yes. I nearly thought that someone might have entered my study without permission,' Leopold said, scratching his head. 'Now where might those things be?' He turned around several times and then looked at Nils uncertainly. 'I'll have to think about this for a moment,' he said apologetically.

'No problem,' Nils replied, trying to control his impatience. Time was flying and he had to leave soon but didn't want to give up when he was so close to success. 'Shall I tidy up a bit, while you concentrate?'

'No, that isn't necessary. Everything is kept in one box.'

'And where might this box be?'

'It's behind the yellow winged chair and has a plant pot on top of it. That way it's not obvious.'

'Very original,' conceded Nils, noticing the flowering orchid on a box. The files had been right under his nose all the time. Why hadn't he spotted it before? Leopold Hofmann really had been a very good psychiatrist. He could make the obvious disappear and make the hidden visible.

'I'll show you the notes. We can go through them together. We cannot afford to make mistakes in the case of such serious allegations.'

'That won't be necessary,' Nils replied. 'The commission will investigate the notes in detail. Please hand them over to me now.'

'Should I really do that?' mumbled Leopold, uncertain. The effect of the drug was slowly wearing off.

'Let me help you,' Nils said, pushing Leopold aside. He picked up the plant pot to place it next to the box on the floor. At the same time Leopold touched his shoulder.

'What are you doing there?'

Nils was startled and dropped the pot, which crashed to the parquet floor with a loud bang. Leopold began to weep and clawed at Nils's shoulder.

'Let go of me,' Nils hissed. He pushed Leopold, who stumbled backwards, fell and hit his head on the floor. Nils opened the box and found several files, fastened together with string.

'Where's the videotape?' He turned around to Leopold, who was lying on his back, confused, his eyes blank. 'The video – where do you keep the video?' Nils shook Leopold's shoulders, but the old man seemed incapable of speech as his head bounced backwards and forwards like that of a ragdoll.

'Damn!' Nils shoved him back with disgust and jumped up. He took the box and turned it upside down. There was nothing left in there. Did this video really exist, or was Leopold fooling him? Out in the stairwell, the lift started to rattle.

'Where's the bloody video?' Nils tried one more time. He grabbed Leopold by the arms and yanked him to his feet. 'Does this video really exist?' he shouted.

'Video? What are you talking about? Of course I have the video. It's here,' Leopold said timidly. He pulled a DVD from the shelf. Nils glanced at it. It was *Fitzcarraldo*.

'That shit film!' Nils hurled the DVD into the corner, then hastily stuffing the paper files into a plastic bag he rushed into the hallway. At that moment he heard the old lift creakingly coming to a standstill. He just managed to get out of the flat by the side entrance and run down the stairs before Olivia stepped out of the lift.

31

Levi tried turning the key but to his surprise found the door unlocked. Carefully he opened it and stepped inside. The old parquet floor creaked. The sight of a figure at the other end of the hallway startled him for a moment, but it was only his own reflection in the large mirror on the far wall. Slowly he went in further. It was quite dark, but he didn't want to switch on the light. There were doors on both sides of the corridor, and he remembered that the study was the first room on the left. The double sliding doors at the end of the corridor stood ajar and a ray of sunlight fell through the gap, cutting through the darkness like a knife. He stopped in front of the wide door reluctantly, knowing that he was not to enter the sitting room: it was private. Finally his curiosity got the better of him and he pushed the door open and stepped inside.

'My God!' Levi took a deep breath. Olivia's sitting room was large and very bright. Specks of dust were dancing in the last rays of the sinking sun that shone in through the large windows. Dotted around the room were exotic plants in large pots and the bay window, looking onto the street below, was alive with colourful flowers. A stack of photo albums sat on a large sofa in the middle of the room. On the far wall were dozens of photos of a small child with blonde hair and pictures of a fair-haired man. Some of the photos had black markings on them. Above the display was the word, 'Why?' written in black paint.

Levi crept closer and stared at a large photo showing Olivia with her husband and child. It seemed to have been taken in happy times, long ago. Olivia had had long curly hair back then. She was smiling. And above that photo, more writing in black: 'Where are you?'

Levi didn't know much about Olivia's family apart from the few bits of information he'd found online. He hadn't liked to pry into what was clearly a private grief. What exactly had happened to her husband and daughter and why had they disappeared? Had they been victims of a crime? Levi realised now why Olivia hadn't wanted him in her sitting room. What he had discovered here was a very personal process of dealing with a loss so terrible that no 'working through' could ever lead to resolution.

Levi found it difficult to pull himself away from the room. He'd come here to find a few files Olivia had taken from the archive and not to snoop around in her flat and private life. He'd promised not to enter the sitting room and now he felt like an intruder.

Feeling guilty he returned to the corridor and entered Olivia's study. It was full of unusual pieces of furniture. Some of the items seemed to have come from South America and behind the desk hung a painting of a colourful jungle city in warm, luminous colours. A tag read '*Casa Caruso, Manaus de Flora*'.

Olivia had said that the files were in a brown envelope on the desk, but all sorts of papers and documents lay scattered over the table.

He searched the drawers and noticed thin scratches on the bottom one. Feeling the wood with his fingertips, it was clear that the marks were fresh. Someone had broken the lock. Carefully he opened the drawer – it was empty. Then he spotted the brown envelope on the floor. Nothing in it. The files were gone.

Suddenly Levi heard something from the room next door. He stood upright, holding his breath. It sounded like an animal moving on soft paws over a tiled floor. Did Olivia have a cat? No, she probably would have mentioned it. Again he heard a hesitant tap-tap-tap. Without a doubt, there was somebody else in the flat.

He sneaked to the door and looked in the corridor. Silence. Then he pushed open the next door. It was the kitchen.

'Hello? Is anybody there?' he called. 'It's OK, I'm a friend of Olivia's. I'm here to get some of her things.' The kitchen floor had black and white tiles like a chessboard. A white table was positioned in front of the window, and on it a colourful vase with fresh flowers. On the worktop, under a shelf with exotic spices, stood a bottle of red wine. *Nobody here*, thought Levi and went in further.

But when he reached the middle of the room, he heard hinges squeak and at the same moment was pushed in the back. Stumbling forward, he instinctively grabbed hold of the table. He turned around and briefly caught a glimpse of a man in a hoodie, with some files under his arm.

'Stop! Police!' Levi shouted, but the stranger ran on.

Levi set off in pursuit. Running was no longer an option with his injured leg, but somehow he kept up and caught the man by the sleeve. With an angry shout the stranger spun around, dropping the files. His face hidden by a scarf and the hood pulled down over his forehead, he pushed Levi back with both hands then lunged for the files on the floor. Levi stumbled backwards, but recovering himself quickly, managed to crawl towards him and grab one of his legs. The man hit Levi repeatedly, but the ex-policeman didn't let go and was instead dragged across the floor to the hallway and the landing outside. Levi's grip loosened, and the stranger pulled free. Somehow, though, Levi managed to grab hold of the files and pull them away. As the man bent down to get them back, Levi shoved him and, stumbling, the intruder tumbled down a few steps before getting up and racing down the rest of the staircase.

'What's all this noise?'

Startled at the sound of the voice behind him, Levi staggered to his feet with a moan. A woman in jeans and T-shirt was standing in front of him, carrying a small child.

'What are you doing in Olivia's flat?' she asked nervously, turning the child around so it couldn't see him.

'Call the police, fast!' Levi said, wiping the blood from his face with the back of his hand. He glanced back to Olivia's flat, then hid the files under his jacket. Relieved, he sat down on the top step to wait for the police to come.

32

The old man was lying on the floor, his breathing shallow. 'Papa, what happened to you?' Ignoring her own discomfort, Olivia knelt next to her father who stared at her wide-eyed. He could only stammer confused words. He was in shock.

'The board has been,' he whispered, grabbing Olivia's arm.

'What board?'

'About the events at the clinic. They want my notes.'

'What events?' asked Olivia. 'Who's been here, Papa? You mentioned a man on the phone. Did you know him?'

'Of course. It was somebody from the board of the clinic. I've been telling you all along.' Carefully Leopold sat up and flattened the creases in his trousers, then rolled down his shirt sleeve. 'What are you doing here in my office?'

'It's your flat, Papa.' Olivia wanted to continue, but then she looked at Leopold's shirt.

'Stop! What's that?' Olivia gently took hold of her father's arm and pointed to the tiny speck of blood on the white shirt. 'Where did that come from? Let me take a look.'

'Don't you touch me!' Leopold pulled his arm back, but Olivia held on tight.

'I need to have a look at that.' She pushed the sleeve up again and saw the needle mark. There was no question about it – someone had injected her father with something. 'Who gave you this injection? Try to remember,' she said, but her father stared blankly over her shoulder, then slowly collapsed. 'Everything is spinning . . .' he stammered.

There were hurried steps outside and minutes later the emergency doctor Olivia had called from the taxi ran in.

'Oh, thank goodness you're here,' Olivia said. 'My father has just collapsed.'

'What on earth happened here?' the doctor asked, staring at the bruising on Olivia's face and the surrounding mess, before kneeling at Leopold's side. 'Was it a robbery?'

'I have no idea.' Olivia shook her head. 'My father has Alzheimer's. He called me because someone was in the flat. He's been injected with something.' She pointed to the needle mark on Leopold's arm.

'I'll take a closer look at it in a minute, but right now your father needs something to stabilise his condition. He's completely disorientated.'

'OK. I'll see whether anything is missing.'

'Have you called the police?' the doctor asked. He checked Leopold's eye response with a torch.

'I was just about to,' Olivia said and dialled for the emergency services. She described what had happened to the call handler at the other end and gave them the address.

'Why should an intruder give your father an injection?' the doctor wondered. 'Are you sure it wasn't your father who messed up the room? Did he have an episode, maybe?'

'He's never been aggressive before. His condition is well controlled,' Olivia said.

'It doesn't look like that to me,' the doctor countered. 'I recommend placing your father in a specialist nursing home for

Alzheimer's patients, where his condition will be stabilised and he can be well cared for.'

'Out of the question,' Olivia said firmly. 'I'm quite capable of looking after him.'

'It was only a recommendation, but he needs a lot of rest right now. Everything else is your decision.'

'Exactly,' Olivia said. 'It is, after all, my choice as to how my father is best looked after.'

Together they helped Leopold up from the floor, Olivia wincing at the pain from her own bruised ribs.

'I'll take him through to the sitting room,' the doctor said as he helped the old man into the corridor.

A while later two policemen entered the flat. Olivia explained what had happened while the policemen took notes.

'Anything missing?' one of them asked.

'Nothing we can see.' Olivia shrugged helplessly.

'Have a good look around and come to the station later to make a statement. Your father is ill?' He exchanged a glance with his colleague.

'He has Alzheimer's,' Olivia answered. She sensed the policemen didn't believe there had been a burglary but suspected the chaos had been caused by her father. 'Thank you for coming so quickly,' she said.

Olivia looked around, wondering. Had her father thrown the files on the floor himself? Or had someone else been in the flat looking for something? She started to put the files back on the shelves so she could try to get a clearer picture of the situation.

Next to the desk she saw the old wooden box with the letters *Manaus* printed on it; lying beside it were pieces of a plant pot and the squashed orchid.

'Surely Papa would never damage a plant that reminds him of Mama,' she whispered. 'Someone has been in here, but what were they looking for?'

She noticed a DVD with a broken case lying in the corner and went to pick it up. *Fitzcarraldo* it said on the faded cover, although Olivia knew the DVD was always in the player.

'Why does Papa have several copies of the same film?' Olivia asked herself. She opened the box and pulled out the DVD. It was not an original, but a copy without a label. Puzzled, Olivia turned it in her hands. It was scratched and cracked. She was about to put it back in its case but then stopped – she needed to check what was on it first.

'I've given your father something to stabilise his circulatory system.' The doctor was back and leaning on the doorframe. 'He's asleep now.'

'Do you have any idea what he might have been injected with?' Olivia asked, looking at him over her shoulder.

'That's a matter for the police. I'll send a blood sample to the laboratory. They'll have the results by next week.'

'Thank you for your help.'

'That's my job. But I do recommend sending your father to a nursing home, at least for tonight,' he said, his expression serious.

'Like I said, my father is staying right here. I'll look after him,' Olivia said.

'Don't take on too much. You don't look exactly fit yourself,' the doctor said, pointing to the bruise on Olivia's temple.

'It was only a bike accident. I'm fine.'

Once the doctor had gone, Olivia slumped on the sofa. She felt drained and miserable, but she had to be strong now. She needed to know what was on that DVD.

The effect of the painkillers was fading, and with every step she felt as though a red-hot poker was stabbing her between the ribs. She gritted her teeth and went over to the DVD player, replacing the original copy of *Fitzcarraldo* with the one from the broken case, then pressed play. Immediately she recognised the person in the film.

It was Lisa. She was sitting on a chair in a neutral room, wearing a white nightgown.

'Take that nightie off,' came a distorted voice from someone off-screen.

Then the film stopped, and all Olivia could see was a flickering white. The DVD was broken. Frustrated she stopped the player. 'How on earth did that DVD come to be in my father's possession?' she wondered.

33

'I just had a brief glance into hell,' Olivia said. Levi had called her but couldn't get a word in first.

'The hell that Lisa was in?' asked Levi.

'There's a damaged DVD showing how Lisa was abused. I can't tell you on the phone. Can you come to my father's flat?'

'Of course. Actually, I'm still in *your* flat right at the moment.'

'What? You're still there?' Olivia tensed up. What in heaven's name could Levi still be doing over there? 'You only went to pick up the files.'

'Someone had broken in,' Levi said. 'I surprised him.'

'A burglar? Are you OK?' Olivia exclaimed anxiously. A stranger had intruded on her very private space? She grew extremely agitated at the thought. And Levi being there and surprising the man!

'I nearly caught the guy. He was after the files in the envelope but luckily I wrenched them off him.'

'Hey, hey, slow down a bit, please.' Olivia took a deep breath. There seemed to be one disaster after the other. First her accident, then her father's messed-up study, and now a break-in at her own flat to steal the files. Clearly their investigations were making someone very nervous. The whole thing was getting increasingly dangerous.

'Well . . . I had to look round your flat with the police, of course' – Levi cleared his throat before carrying on – 'so I went into your sitting room and saw the photos. You can talk to me whenever you feel like it.'

'That's what psychiatrists are for,' Olivia replied curtly. What the hell did Levi think of her now – that she was completely mad? She could justify herself easily enough: the photos on the walls were her way of dealing with her terrible loss. When she talked to the photos, her family were alive for her again. 'But thank you anyway,' she added.

'Sometimes it's better to talk to a friend,' Levi said quietly.

'Are you my friend then?'

'Yes, I am.'

Levi's voice had a very calming effect on Olivia, and she believed him.

'I'll text you my father's address,' she said abruptly, ending the call.

She started to clear up, every now and then checking on her father who was sleeping soundly. A short time later the doorbell rang, and Levi was standing there, a creased envelope in his hand.

'My God, what happened to you?' Olivia put a hand in front of her mouth in shock.

'I got into a fight over you,' Levi replied with a wry smile. When he entered the hallway, Olivia noticed that he was limping slightly.

'What's the matter with your leg?'

'The guy whacked it,' Levi answered as if it were nothing and waved the envelope at her. 'This is Lisa's patient file.'

With Levi there to reassure her, Olivia was feeling better already. Maybe one day she'd talk to him about the disappearance of her family, but not just yet.

'Very smart,' Levi said as he looked around the flat. 'Why don't you live here in the Ninth District? It's a desirable area and not far from your office.'

'You must be joking,' Olivia said, shaking her head. 'Living with my father and then maybe ending up as a single woman for the rest of my life?' Then, in a more serious tone, she added, 'Anyway, apart from that, I already had a family of my own and a life.' She stopped herself and added, 'Ah, just forget it.'

She took Levi into the large sitting room with the fantastic view of the Votivkirche.

'Take a look at this video,' she said, pressing play. 'It's only a few seconds but tells you a lot.'

They sat on the floor and played the short sequence several times over. The image of the fragile-looking Lisa with her huge, sad eyes was seared on their brains.

'What a monster,' Levi said. 'Who's that talking to her? Is the voice familiar to you? Or the room?'

'It's one of the treatment rooms, I'm sure, but it could be anywhere at the clinic.'

'Short as it is, this film clearly shows somebody exploiting Lisa's situation but unless we know who the other person is, it doesn't help much.' Levi stood up slowly and went over to sit down at the large dining table.

'I think the film proves a lot though,' Olivia said, with a questioning look. 'You can see very clearly how Lisa was being manipulated and then probably abused, certainly by a doctor.'

'That's merely an assumption because you can't tell from the film who the other person is,' Levi said, 'and the voice is distorted.'

'No good then,' Olivia said, biting her knuckles. 'Do you think it would be possible to find out when the video was made? Maybe a technician could analyse the recording so the voice can be recognised.'

'The DVD is cracked and very scratched. There's nothing you can do with it,' Levi said, dampening her hopes. 'Maybe there's something in her file that would give us a clue.'

'Good idea,' Olivia replied with renewed enthusiasm. 'Where do we start?'

'Let's look first at the days leading up to Lisa's disappearance,' Levi suggested.

Silently they read through the notes. Clearly, Lisa had been in one particular treatment room several times with Nils Wagner.

'My father told me already that Lisa was under Nils's care,' Olivia said, 'but when I spoke to Nils, he pretended not to remember her. I knew then he was lying.'

'I only got as far as questioning the duty doctor before I was injured and I don't remember there being an interview with Nils Wagner in the transcripts,' Levi said, 'but I'll take another look at my files, just to be sure.'

'Here's another interesting detail,' Olivia said, pointing to a line in the notes. 'Lisa did some therapy with a student doctor – which goes strictly against hospital protocol.'

They continued to study the file quietly, but nothing else of particular significance leapt out at them.

'Right, and now we come to the night when Lisa disappeared,' Levi said, turning over a folded page.

'Nurse Emma Kern was on night duty,' Olivia read aloud. 'Ah, she still works on that ward. I can easily ask her.'

'Hang on, what was the name of that nurse again?'

'Emma Kern.'

'Strange,' Levi said, scratching his stubble. 'If I remember correctly from my own files, she told us she'd not been working on Lisa Manz's ward at the time.'

'But it states it very clearly here,' Olivia said. 'What a total bunch of lies! No one is telling the truth.' She was exhausted and propped her chin on her fists. 'It's so depressing!'

'No, not at all,' Levi said in encouragement. 'We have evidence here of a witness who obviously lied. We'll need to question her again.'

'I have something else that might help – how could I have forgotten?' Gingerly Olivia got to her feet, went into the hallway and came back with her bag. 'Jonathan gave me this item of jewellery in our last session together.' She pulled the pendant from the bag and showed it to Levi. 'He was afraid of it. The snakes with their red eyes really scared him.'

'What an unusual piece,' Levi said as he took it from Olivia's hand. 'It does look a little spooky,' he concluded after inspecting it thoroughly.

'I did wonder how a fourteen-year-old girl might have got hold of such a valuable ornament.' Olivia wrapped the leather strap around her fingers and dangled the pendant in front of Levi's face.

'Are you going to hypnotise me?' he asked. 'Maybe it's an heirloom on Theresa's side, the Stollwerks, passed on from mother to daughter.'

'Or Lisa got it from her murderer,' Olivia said, thinking aloud.

'Let's start with Lisa's family and show it to Theresa Manz tomorrow. I'll ask if it ever belonged to her, while you observe her reaction.'

'Why?'

'Because most people lie.'

34

The driveway up to the Villa Manz was designed to hide the place from view until the very last moment. Olivia was not impressed by its overblown country house aesthetic.

'You again,' Theresa Manz said, wafting down the stone steps in a Moroccan kaftan. 'Oh, and who have you brought along today?' she asked, pointing to Olivia. 'Is this your assistant?'

'This is Doctor Hofmann, a psychiatrist,' Levi said, gesturing to Olivia not to say a word.

'Do you want to section me?' Theresa flashed her teeth in an offhand smile and then turned her back on them. 'You're a little late – I already live in the biggest madhouse in Vienna.' She walked off through the entrance hall towards the large drawing room.

'We don't want to bother you for long, Frau Manz,' Levi started calmly. 'I only have one question for you today.'

'Good, because my husband will be back soon, and he doesn't like it when there are ex-coppers sneaking around.'

'Do you recognise this pendant?' Olivia asked, coming straight out with it and taking over from Levi. She pulled the piece of jewellery from her bag and showed it to Theresa. She immediately regretted having acted so hastily and noticed an irritated glance from Levi. Olivia often struggled with her impulsiveness and silently vowed to control herself from now on. Theresa Manz stretched her hand out for the piece, but Olivia held on to it. 'It's evidence,' she said.

'What do you mean, evidence?' Theresa gave her a puzzled look.

'Did this pendant belong to your daughter?' Levi said.

'Why are you asking me that? I don't understand,' Theresa murmured. 'The case is closed, isn't it? The murderer committed suicide – my husband told me. Is that not true?'

'Generally speaking, he's quite correct,' Levi said, 'only there are a few questions still outstanding.'

'Have you ever seen this pendant before?' Olivia interrupted, ignoring Levi's warning glance. 'You only have to answer with a yes or a no.'

'Can I have another look, please?' Theresa asked, and suddenly Olivia sensed some insecurity in the other woman. *You just have to be a bit harder with her and she crumbles.*

'Of course.'

Olivia gave the pendant to Theresa who looked at it carefully.

'No, I've never seen it before, but it's certainly a beautiful item of jewellery. Those rubies are very valuable. Where did you find it?' She frowned. 'But why would you think it was Lisa's?'

'We're not at liberty to reveal that information.' Levi gave her a noncommittal smile.

'Don't be ridiculous. You aren't even with the police any more,' Theresa said. 'And you failed utterly when you were tasked with finding the person who murdered my daughter. Is your conscience haunting you now?'

'So you don't recognise this pendant?' Olivia said, noticing Levi's face muscles twitch, although he otherwise ignored Theresa's accusations; she admired his composure. But the other woman's reaction was telling for Olivia. Theresa herself seemed haunted by a guilty conscience, which she was projecting onto others.

'I've never seen this pendant before in my life,' Theresa repeated, before rising from the large sofa and going over to the richly carved dresser. 'All these questions are making me rather thirsty,' she muttered, pouring herself a glass of champagne. She drained the glass in one gulp and refilled it immediately, then she looked Levi and Olivia up and down. 'Anything else? As I said, my husband will be here any minute.'

'Has he been away on a business trip?' asked Levi.

'No, he's been with his mistress,' Theresa said and turned away. 'He always comes back in the mornings,' she whispered, as though to herself.

'Why is it that you could never love your daughter?' asked Olivia. 'Mothers love their children normally.'

'Is this turning into a therapy session?' Theresa turned the stem of the glass between her fingers. 'Lisa destroyed my life. I wanted a career, but Richard insisted I stay at home while she was little because you can't combine childcare with being an actor.'

'But you could have tried,' Olivia suggested. 'I'm sure you could have afforded a nanny?'

'Of course, but Richard was against it. He didn't want strangers living in the house. He fears losing control. You don't know my husband – everything must go his way; he wants total power. He tried imposing that on Lisa too, but my daughter was stronger than me. She resisted him. She didn't agree with his ideas of discipline and obedience, so he shuffled her off to the clinic.' Theresa fell silent and pulled her kaftan tighter around her body. 'I've talked to you for long enough now. Sorry if I bored you with my story.'

'Not at all,' Olivia countered. All of a sudden, she was seeing Theresa in a different light. The arrogant actor was really a deeply insecure woman who was being terrorised by her husband. 'Maybe you'd like to talk to someone about this,' she suggested.

'Good advice, but I'm not in need of a psychiatrist at this precise moment,' Theresa said coldly. 'Maybe one day the right time will come and I'll tell my story,' she added, 'but now you'll have to forgive me. I have more important things to do than chat with you.' Theresa slipped straight back into the role of arrogant actor.

'Thank you for your time, Frau Manz. We'll find our own way out.' Levi gave Theresa a friendly nod and took Olivia's arm.

Shortly before the huge entrance door they heard Theresa say behind them, 'That pendant is an art deco piece, I'm sure of it. Try Gina's Jewellery Workshop in the Eighth District. Gina's a very talented jewellery designer – she knows many artists and their respective dealers. I'm sure she'd be able to help you with this.'

35

LISA'S DIARY

I'm to meet the doctor again today.

'Take your clothes off,' he says, and the game starts all over again. It lasts a long time, until I develop some feelings. His hand grabs me between my legs, and he's filming my face.

'What are you feeling? Describe the thoughts going through your head.'

'I want this to stop,' I say and imagine what it's like to be dead.

How lovely it must be to lie in a coffin, in deep, deep silence. No hands to touch me, no sounds. Black earth surrounding me. I will sleep and wake up again in an unknown country.

'That's not good enough.' His voice sounds regretful. 'You know I'm only trying to help you. Everything I'm doing is in your best interests. I like you.'

'Then stop.'

'And what do I get if I close your case?' he asks, a subtle threat in his voice.

A ray of light in the darkest night. It's my chance, and I have to take it.

'I won't tell anyone at home,' I whisper, and realise immediately that this is the wrong answer. The doctor grins and grabs me by the neck.

'Are you threatening me?' he asks, and I feel his breath on my face. 'I'm going to have to punish you for that.'

He grabs me harder and presses me down on the chair, binding me to the armrests with the leather straps so I can't move. Then he takes a syringe from the table and slowly walks towards me before jabbing it into my arm. A dangerous tiredness washes over me, then he loosens the straps and everything becomes blurred. Something is happening to me, but I have no idea what it is.

When it's over and I'm back in my sweatshirt and joggers, I stay several more minutes in the doctor's room. He silently writes his notes, then looks at me for a long time.

'Have you been having sexual fantasies again, Lisa?'

'Those weren't fantasies. They were real,' I say and feel the tears burning in my eyes. 'What have you done to me, you bastard?' I shout at him, louder and louder. I jump up and launch myself across the desk, but the doctor ducks to the side. My fists punch at thin air.

'Still so aggressive,' he says, shaking his head.

He presses a button. Seconds later two nurses enter the room and take me between them. Outside is a man I've never seen before.

'This is Lisa,' the doctor says to the man. 'Begin the behavioural therapy sessions with her.'

'Will you participate?' the man asks.

'I'll check on her progress now and then.'

'Are you a doctor?' I ask the man.

'I'm still a student. I'm doing my traineeship here,' he answers. 'Let's take you to your room.'

Slowly we walk along the corridor. There's soft, calming music coming from the loudspeakers, and together with the hospital smells of antiseptic and cleanliness here, it's making me sleepy.

'That doctor always make me undress,' I whisper when we're back in my room.

'Tell me more about it.' The student takes a black notebook from his pocket and starts writing. I tell him everything about the doctor and his games. The student patiently writes it all down.

'Do you believe me?' I say as I sink back on my bed, exhausted.

'Of course I believe you.' The student pats my arm and looks at me sympathetically. 'Tomorrow we'll start working together, so you'll be able to stand up to the doctor.'

But the student is lying.

During the night the doctor comes into my room to ask how I'm feeling.

'What did you tell the student, Lisa?' he asks, pushing up my nightie. 'Why aren't you wearing any knickers?' He kneads my buttocks. 'You'll catch a cold.'

The student comes every day now and I tell him what happens in the night with the doctor. He writes everything down in his notebook, then starts asking questions about my parents and why I'm always so aggressive.

'Let's play a game,' he says one day.

He takes two cushions and puts them on the two chairs in my room.

'Imagine those two cushions are your parents,' he says. 'Now tell them everything you don't like about them.'

It takes a while, but then the words come spewing out of my mouth. The cushions are real people – they become Mama and Papa. Towards the end I'm flinging myself at them, thumping them with both fists. Then he takes me in his strong arms and holds me very tight.

It feels good, to be held like that. I feel safe with the student.

36

They found Gina's Jewellery Workshop in a former printing office, tucked down a quiet side street in the Eighth District. Levi pulled up in the Saab right outside.

'Seems pretty rundown around here for a jeweller's workshop,' Levi said. Inside, extravagant pieces of jewellery were mounted on velvet-covered printing rollers and in lettering cases to enhance their appearance.

'What can I do for you?' The woman's hair was dyed a shocking shade of red.

'A customer of yours, Theresa Manz, sent us here,' Levi said, introducing Olivia and himself.

'Oh, the lovely, ever-so-sensitive Theresa.' Olivia was not entirely sure whether Gina was being ironic. 'How can I help you?'

'Have you ever come across this piece?' Olivia pulled the pendant from her bag and placed it on a counter converted from an antique printing press.

'What a beautiful ornament!' Gina studied the pendant thoughtfully. 'Yes, those snakes with their flickering tongues somehow seem familiar. Maybe it's from the Naschmarkt flea market.'

'You'd surely not find such a precious item at a flea market?' Levi said.

'On the contrary – plenty of dealers there specialise in art deco antiques,' Gina said.

'Can you remember which dealer might have been offering it?' asked Olivia.

'No, but there aren't that many people who deal with high-end art deco pieces. I can jot down their names for you.'

'That would be wonderful,' Olivia said and turned to Levi. 'It'll be a big step forward when we find out where Lisa got hold of this piece.'

Gina brought them the list and they said their goodbyes.

'Maybe we should split up,' Levi said as they walked back to his car. 'I'll try to contact Emma Kern, and confront her with that lie. Maybe she'll tell the truth this time.'

'And in the meantime, I'll go and visit the antique shops on that list and ask whether anybody remembers seeing the pendant before.'

'Where's your bike? Didn't the police take it in after your accident?'

'Simon brought it over to my office. He even repaired the damage,' Olivia said. When she'd taken the taxi to her father's flat that evening, she'd called Simon and asked him to bring the bike round to her office. She hadn't expected him to repair her light and the front tyre as well, and Olivia had not had time to thank him for it.

'Simon? Who's Simon?' asked Levi.

'Simon Berger is a junior doctor at the clinic,' Olivia said. 'I went to the cinema with him recently.'

'Ah.' Levi said, nothing more. Olivia glanced at him quickly, but his face was inscrutable.

'Just let me out here, will you?' Olivia asked as they drove along Währinger Strasse. 'I'd like to walk a bit and mull things over.'

She still didn't feel quite right as she slowly walked along Bergstrasse towards her office. She'd already cancelled all appointments for the week because she wasn't sure whether the board of the clinic would raise concerns and suspend her. Once in her office she took a couple of painkillers and looked online for the addresses of the antique shops from Gina's list, then printed them out and studied the directions.

Simon had left her bicycle in the shady backyard, and when Olivia pushed it towards the street, she could feel her bruised ribs despite the painkillers. *Maybe going by bike isn't such a great idea*, she thought, but gritted her teeth and got on with it.

Olivia spent the afternoon cycling from one shop to the next without success. She tried contacting Levi several times to express her frustration, but he didn't answer.

By the time she was cycling along Praterstrasse, she was exhausted. There were two more shops left on her list, and she couldn't help wondering whether there was much point in visiting them, given the lack of success she'd had at the others. The shop on Praterstrasse was called 'Paradise Lost' and occupied the whole ground floor of one of the old Viennese palaces. When Olivia entered through the high double doors, it was like stepping into a realm of magic and fantasy. The shop was the size of a ballroom with a thirty-foot-high ceiling, its walls covered with antique mirrors which reflected and distorted her image as well as the items on display. Despite its size, the room appeared small as it was crammed full with carriages, suits of armour, tables, sofas, wardrobes and statues.

'Hello, is anybody there?' Olivia called, but there was no answer.

A small strip was kept clear down the middle of the room, although Olivia still had to fight her way between old coats and robes towards the back. She came to another, smaller room, separated from the salesroom by tall, richly decorated glazed doors. Beyond, she saw an empty desk with an open cupboard behind it.

Olivia hesitated for a moment, then pressed the door handle. As she did so, a hand fell on her shoulder and she jumped back, startled.

'That room is private,' a quiet voice said behind her. She turned around and found herself looking at a well-groomed man in a black suit.

'Oh dear, you gave me quite a shock!' Olivia said, taking a deep breath.

'I'm Frederick, the owner.' The man scrutinised Olivia. 'Have you had a fall?' he asked, pointing to the bruise on her temple.

'A silly bicycle accident,' Olivia replied with an embarrassed smile.

'Well, cycling can be dangerous. What can I do for you?' He flashed a charming smile. He came across as an easy-going man of the world – a touch out of place in the midst of this chaotic emporium.

'Gina from the jewellery workshop gave me your address. I'd like to ask your advice if that's possible.'

'Oh, Gina. How nice of her. What's this all about then?'

'Has this ever come your way before?' Olivia said, showing Frederick the pendant.

'May I?' Frederick asked politely, taking it from her hand. 'What a beautiful piece,' he said as he studied it, then after some deliberation dangled the precious item in Olivia's face. 'Yes, I know this design from one of my own objects, but I'll have to look it up. As you can see, I'm nearly drowning in my treasure trove,' he said apologetically.

'You'd be doing me a huge favour if you could take a look. I'll walk around here in the meantime – might even find a present for my father. His birthday's coming up,' Olivia said as she tucked the pendant back in her bag. 'How do you know Gina?' she asked

157

as they struggled through the coats and dresses back to the front showroom.

'Gina sold some heirlooms for me,' Frederick said, 'and by and by we became friends. Now she sends me customers every now and then, so I can keep all this up.' He pointed to the high ceiling. 'The maintenance costs here are enormous.'

'Why don't you rent a smaller place?' asked Olivia.

'I promised my parents to keep on at the palace – it's been in the family since 1693 and it's worth fighting for.'

'You're right,' Olivia said. 'Are your parents still alive?'

'My father died a long time ago, and my mother went downhill after that. There wasn't a week when I didn't have to take her to the psychiatric clinic. She gave up the battle last year.'

'I'm so sorry to hear that. That's very sad.' Then, acting on a hunch, Olivia asked, 'Have you ever heard the name Lisa Manz?'

'Lisa? Oh yes, that poor girl who was murdered five years ago,' Frederick said. 'I did see the police at the clinic at the time but there wasn't a lot of information. Everything seemed to have been swept under the carpet.'

'But you never met Lisa personally?'

'No. Why are you asking me all these questions – did the pendant belong to Lisa?'

'Maybe,' Olivia said evasively.

Frederick disappeared to the back of the showroom, while Olivia wandered off through the small spaces between the piles of leather-bound books and ancient board games.

Just then one of the items on display caught her attention. She'd not noticed it before among all the jumble. It was a huge mirror, decorated with faded trompe l'oeil paintwork, leaning against a wall. Slowly she walked towards it. The silvery surface of the glass was stained with black flecks, but the decoration of the frame was familiar. It showed two snakes, their heads meeting at the top of the mirror, their slithering tongues touching. The eyes were of a luminous, malicious red.

Olivia touched the frame and pulled the pendant from her bag. It was exactly the same motif. The mirror and the pendant had been designed by the same artist. A shadow appeared in the stained mirror, and spinning around, she found Frederick advancing on her, fixing her with his stare.

37

Levi was standing in line in the kosher butcher's shop near the Karmelitermarkt. He'd decided to observe the Jewish tradition and celebrate Sabbath again with Rebecca, even though they were not very religious. Maybe sitting over a relaxed meal on a Friday evening he'd be able to talk to her about what was driving him to continue investigations into the Lisa Manz case. Their marriage was on the rocks, but he still loved his wife and hoped he could help her to understand.

'I'd like a good piece of meat for Friday, please,' Levi told the butcher, an orthodox Jew with long sidelocks and a kippa on his head.

'Do you have any particular preference?'

'A nice slab of beef, please,' Levi said, watching as the butcher noted it down in his large order book.

Pleased with his plan, he lingered for a moment outside the shop until recalling his mission to meet the nurse, Emma Kern. She'd obviously lied during the police inquiry five years ago and Levi needed to know why. He grabbed his mobile.

'I'd like to talk to ward sister Emma Kern,' he said when the receptionist of the clinic answered.

After a moment, a soft female voice said, 'Yes, Nurse Emma here.'

'Frau Kern, my name is Levi Kant, from the police. I'd like to ask you a few questions?'

'What about?' she asked warily.

'It's concerning a case from five years ago.'

'Ah, you're probably referring to the Lisa Manz case,' Emma said immediately. 'I told the police everything I knew at the time. There's nothing else to say. If you'll excuse me now, I'm on duty.'

'No, Frau Kern, that's where you're wrong – there's a lot to explain. For example, I came across your name in the patient's file and the entry refers to the night when Lisa disappeared from the clinic.' Levi heard Emma breathing hard before she answered.

'I can't tell you anything else.'

Levi wanted to ask more, but Emma cut the call.

OK, thought Levi. *In which case I'll go to the clinic and talk to you personally.*

But before that he needed to drop in at another certain place in the Second District. As he walked past the flower shop on Karmelitermarkt, Moses, the shopkeeper, waved at him.

'Levi, I've not seen you at all this week.'

'I had a lot on. And I had to correct the essays of my final year students. The semester is over now.'

'You look tense, my friend – like when you were still with the police.'

'I'm helping a friend with a difficult situation.' Levi didn't want to go into detail and changed the subject. 'You have the usual flowers?' he asked.

'Of course. I knew you'd come.' Moses pulled a large bunch of wildflowers from a bucket. 'Simple and beautiful, like you always ask for.'

'These flowers are hardy,' Levi said. 'They grow on the roadside, are trampled on and still come into flower again and again. That is real toughness.'

'Never give up. Keep on flowering, like God wants it.'

'Don't talk to me about God,' Levi said. 'He didn't help me five years ago.'

'God is not your employee, Levi, He only shows you the way, but it is you who has to walk it. You took the wrong road back then, and fate punished you,' Moses said.

'Maybe you're right. I'll be observing the Sabbath again this week for the first time in a long while. With Rebecca. Maybe it will be good for our marriage.'

'See, Levi, now you seem to be on the right path.' Moses nodded approvingly.

'I hope so. Till next time.' Levi raised his hand in farewell and left the shop.

His mobile rang but he didn't recognise the number.

'I'm on duty for another hour. Can we meet afterwards at my house? I don't want to make a fuss at the clinic,' Emma Kern said, notably cool.

'Yes, that should be possible.'

'The lies have to stop now. See you in an hour.' Emma told him her address and ended the call.

Levi, bunch of flowers under one arm, crossed the Karmelitermarkt and turned into a side street, where the Saab was parked. He drove off along Praterstrasse towards Praterstern.

Here the atmosphere changed and was no longer calm and peaceful. Despite a visible police presence, this was the city's main drug-dealing area. Rival gangs clashed frequently, often using weapons to fight it out.

Five years ago, while attempting to make an arrest, Levi had been caught in crossfire between rival Albanian and Russian mafia gangs, battling for control of the local cocaine market. A stray bullet had hit him as he was crossing the bleak and windswept space, bang in the middle of the Lisa Manz case. And all of a sudden, he himself had come face to face with his own mortality. The bullet had hit an artery and he'd lost a lot of blood. His chances of survival had been slim but he'd battled on and returned to life. He hadn't given up. Just like those wildflowers. Now, in bright daylight, everything appeared peaceful and non-threatening. Young people were hanging out on the benches, pensioners were feeding the pigeons.

He placed the flowers at the foot of a concrete wall and walked on quickly. This was his weekly ritual and not even Rebecca knew about it.

An hour later he was walking towards the terraced house where Emma Kern lived.

'You haven't changed,' Emma said as she opened the door.

'We've never met before,' Levi answered with a puzzled look.

'I read in the papers about the Lisa Manz case and saw a photo of you at the time,' Emma continued, trying to conceal her nervousness.

'What would you like to tell me?' Levi said, cutting to the chase as he sat down on the sofa in the cluttered sitting room.

He stole a few glances around while waiting for an answer. Dozens of glass horses in all possible postures and sizes stood on little casual tables. A strange huffing and whistling came from the room next door, as if from bellows.

'Yes, there's something you should know,' Emma finally managed after a long silence. 'I was on duty that night.'

'The night of Lisa Manz's disappearance?' Levi said in confirmation. 'Please go on.'

'Lisa was totally beside herself when she came back from the therapy session. She wouldn't stop crying and said over and over that she wanted to kill herself. I felt so sorry for her.'

'Did you inform her therapist?'

'No, but I had my reasons.' Emma picked up one of the glass horses and held it against the light. 'A lovely piece of work. Bohemian crystal. I often show it to my son – he likes it.'

'So what happened then?'

'I didn't lock the doors like I usually did so she could escape.'

'What? Lisa escaped all on her own? How was that possible?'

'Somebody helped her,' Emma said.

'Do you know who?'

'No, sorry. I was busy in the staffroom at the time with a patient who was upset but I did see two people through the window.'

'And when you returned you noticed that Lisa had gone,' Levi said.

'Yes.'

'The police weren't called until three days later,' Levi remembered from the case file. 'When did you inform your superiors?'

'The next day, but the management wanted to keep the whole thing as quiet as possible.' Emma fell silent. Levi pricked up his ears, realising that the strange sounds had stopped next door.

'Excuse me, please,' Emma said, getting up quickly. She opened the door and went into the next room. Levi rose and peered in. A young man was lying on a high hospital bed, only his arms and his head free of the blankets that enveloped him. A plastic mask sat on his face, connected to a breathing apparatus. The balloon was deflating and inflating rhythmically – the source of the hissing sound Levi had heard through the wall.

'This is my son, Florian,' Emma said when she noticed Levi standing behind her. 'He has locked-in syndrome.' She stroked the boy's forehead. 'It was a simple car accident. He only had a slight concussion. Two days later he collapsed – a blood clot on the brain. I've been looking after him since then, along with my sister.'

'I am so sorry,' Levi said.

'The bed and the machines cost thousands of euros,' Emma said, 'more than I could earn in ten years. The insurance company hasn't helped so far. The board of the clinic made me an offer and I took it.'

'So you were told to make a false statement,' Levi concluded. 'But why?'

'The members of the board went to look for Lisa themselves,' Emma said. 'They wanted to find her without involving the police. In return for my statement they supplied me with the bed and the machines – for free.'

'I can understand why you did it,' Levi said. He had already decided not to tell anyone about Emma's false statement.

'Really?' Emma's voice trembled.

'Yes, but one last question. Who was it who made you that offer?'

'It was Nils Wagner.'

38

'The snake mirror came from a customer in Burgenland,' Frederick told Olivia. They were sitting in Frederick's office. Dozens of files lay spread across the desk, but Frederick couldn't find the name of the person who had sold him the mirror.

'It wasn't me who took the mirror in,' he said shrugging, 'and it's all a very long time ago.'

'Do you have an address maybe?'

'I'll have another look in the archive.' Frederick went over to a shabby old trunk.

'You think it's in there?' Olivia asked, puzzled. The trunk was full to the brim with notes, bills and envelopes.

'There is a certain system to it,' Frederick explained and winked at her. Then he knelt down and rummaged around before eventually pulling out a creased sheet of paper.

'Voilà!' he exclaimed. 'Here's the address.' Then he looked at the note more closely. 'It is a little faded, I'm afraid – it's quite old.'

'What a shame,' murmured the disappointed Olivia.

'I can definitely make out the word "Burgenland" though – why don't you head there?' Frederick said. 'A nice little trip to Lake Neusiedel. Might be lovely.'

'I don't have the time,' Olivia said regretfully. *It would have been too easy if I'd found the owner straight away*, she thought ruefully.

She took a photo of the mirror and said goodbye to Frederick. Again she tried contacting Levi but only got through to his voice-mail. With a sigh she dialled the number of the person looking after her father.

'How is my father?' she asked.

'I've finally had a good talk with him,' the woman said.

'What about? Has something happened?' Olivia became anxious again.

'This can't go on. Your father has to go into a home.'

'What are you saying?' Olivia was getting angry.

'You understand me perfectly well, Frau Doctor.' The woman's voice was icy.

It was pointless trying to discuss this any further on the phone. 'I'll come over now so we can talk about it.'

A short time later she was standing in the large flat and looking down on two huge suitcases dappled with hotel stickers from bygone times. They were Flora and Leopold's luggage, which had been stored in the attic ever since the two of them had come back from Brazil.

'What are the bags doing here?' Olivia asked. The woman who looked after her father came in from the kitchen, a dishcloth in her hand.

'Your father's packed already. He's agreed to move into a home. Today,' the woman said, folding her arms in front of her chest.

'What on earth did he do?'

'He took all the milk and juice cartons from the fridge and emptied them on the floor, then got undressed and lay down in the puddle. "A bath for me and my Flora", he said.'

'Is that really so bad?' Olivia asked.

'It took me hours to clean him up in the shower and to sort out the kitchen,' the woman complained.

'And where is he now?' Olivia was finding it difficult to keep her composure, although she had to admit the woman was probably right, and her anger subsided. She knew how difficult Leopold could be when he suffered one of his episodes, but was it really necessary to scold the old man so much that he was willing to go into a home?

'He's in his study.'

Olivia went along the corridor and opened the door to find her father sitting on a pile of books, tears pouring down his face. He was holding the crudely repaired plant pot with the broken stem of Flora's orchid. When he saw Olivia, he turned his back on her. 'I don't want to go. You want to get rid of me. I am to disappear from your life,' he whispered.

'What absolute nonsense! I will never leave you alone and I will always stay with you. You can go and unpack those suitcases right now.' Olivia had to swallow hard.

'But the angry woman said I have to go into a home; it can't go on like this,' Leopold said.

'It can't go on like this,' Olivia whispered. The words echoed around her mind, and she felt a burning pain in her head. She remembered the evening of her daughter's birthday party.

After their bath, Olivia and Juli dressed up for the occasion.

'What's the matter with Papa?'

'Wait a moment, darling,' Olivia said and took her daughter to her room.

Worried, she went looking for Michael and found him still lying on the sofa in the sitting room.

'Come on, pull yourself together. It's Juli's birthday. Did you get the present? Is it wrapped in pink paper? She'll be so excited when she sees the Barbie,' Olivia whispered.

'No, I didn't do it,' an exhausted Michael said.

'Why not? Where is it? I'll wrap it. There's still time.'

'I'm sorry. I spent the money gambling and all our savings are gone too. I was so very close to winning but it wasn't to be. I'm sorry – I'm such a loser.'

'It can't go on like this, Michael. I can't stand it any more!'

How much she regretted having said that. How she'd love to go back in time and change everything. But it was too late.

39

Nils Wagner put the receiver back and reflected on the phone call. He'd just talked to a porter at the clinic, and what the man had told him was unsettling.

'What's wrong?' asked the man sitting in front of Nils's desk.

Nils had met up with him to explore the next steps. Earlier he'd shredded all of Leopold Hofmann's incriminating material against him and for a short time had felt able to relax. The other man was now looking at him expectantly.

'That ex-policeman Levi Kant is still stirring up the old case.'

'Nothing new about that,' the man replied, raising his eyebrows. 'What makes you so nervous about it?'

'He's been to see Emma Kern,' Nils said. 'One of the porters here overheard her phone conversation with him.'

'She won't say anything, will she?' the man questioned nervously. 'Why is he questioning her again after all this time?'

'He probably read the patient file and found something.'

'How can he have? How did he get hold of the confidential file? They're covered by data protection laws!' The man was getting angry.

'Kant is very persistent,' Nils said with a resigned smile. 'And he's not working alone. A psychiatrist is helping him. I've put her under a bit of pressure, but she's equally stubborn. She probably stole the file from our archive.'

'You could take her to court for that.'

'No, we can't prove it and it would make too much noise, but she'll be stopped soon. The board will take action against her. I'm working on it.'

'Who is this woman anyway?' The man sounded irritated.

'Olivia Hofmann,' Nils answered. 'She's a very good psychiatrist.'

'Hofmann? Don't tell me she's Leopold Hofmann's daughter? The renowned psychiatrist?'

'Exactly. She had an accident recently and was in hospital.'

'So she's no danger to us at the moment?'

'Yes, she is. She discharged herself.'

'Damn. Sounds like she won't give up.'

'Our past is catching up with us.' Nils drummed his fingers nervously on his thighs.

'Rubbish. It's all Lisa's fault. She was evil – always playing these little games. That's why she needed to be controlled and punished. The problem was, you allowed yourself to be taken in by her sweet little face.'

'No, it wasn't like that,' Nils said, remembering back to the fragile young girl with the large eyes. Why had it all turned out this way? Why did Lisa have to be referred to his clinic? And why had he developed such strong feelings for her? He wished he could turn back the clock and do everything differently, but it was too late now. Once you're in league with the devil, he won't let you go. You sink deeper and deeper into the mire. Until you drown.

'How is it that Olivia is still allowed to work as a psychiatrist?' The man's words pulled him back from the darkness. 'I thought you were going to suspend her?'

'Her office is closed. I checked that.'

'Didn't you say that her husband and daughter disappeared years ago? It might be a good idea to remind the board about that. Maybe she has something to do with her family's disappearance?'

'Would you really go that far?' Nils asked. 'It would ruin her life altogether to suggest something like that.'

'Of course. Before she ruins ours,' the man answered coldly.

'So what's our next step?' Nils asked. He was exhausted, at the end of his tether. He'd love to go to the police and tell them everything.

'I'll see to it that the unauthorised actions of this ex-copper are put a stop to by the head of police, and you see to it that Olivia Hofmann stops snooping around.'

'I've already talked to the head of police, but it doesn't seem to have had any effect.'

'Because you don't know how to put people under pressure, Nils,' the other man said condescendingly. 'I'll take that in hand now.'

'Just don't forget this Kant is a real terrier after the truth.'

'What are you talking about? Kant is no threat to us. He's as good as dead already,' Richard Manz said, rising from his chair, his thin lips curled into the semblance of a smile.

40

Levi was standing in front of his filing cabinet, fidgeting. From the living room he could hear Rebecca's voice as she patiently told one of her pupils about Chopin's life. He smiled. Rebecca was very good at making her lessons even more interesting by telling her students these stories.

As the first of Chopin's études began to drift into the room, Levi gave himself a kick and opened the cabinet. He'd been through all but one of the files. With a sigh he took out the one labelled 'Non-relevant witness statements' and sat down at his desk.

Lovely music playing in the background, he went through the notes. A few days after Lisa had disappeared from the clinic there'd been a missing person appeal in the media. More than a dozen people had contacted them, claiming to have seen Lisa. Most of the statements had turned out to be false trails, but one of them had caught Levi's interest. A witness had seen a blonde girl walking from Ruster Bay on Lake Neusiedel towards the station. The description of the girl fitted Lisa, and the local police had found the girl before she caught the train to Vienna.

'What's your name?'

'My name is Birgit Stöger.'

'And where do you live?'

'In Vienna. Tenth District.'

'What are you doing here?'

'I've been to visit my friend Nils.'

Levi frowned and thought hard. According to the statement the girl had had a striking resemblance to Lisa Manz. And then there was this friend Nils.

Levi took his mobile and dialled the number listed in the file for Birgit Stöger. He just hoped it was still working. He was lucky. She answered immediately.

'I need some information,' Levi said, after he'd introduced himself as a policeman.

'What's this about?' Birgit asked reluctantly.

'Five years ago, you were in Ruster Bay with your friend Nils.'

'Yes,' Birgit answered haltingly.

'What is Nils's surname?'

'It was five years ago. I can't remember,' the young woman replied.

'You can't remember your friend's surname?' Levi said.

'He wasn't my friend, only an acquaintance.'

'Now listen to me. This is concerning a murder. If you won't tell me this guy's surname, then you're obstructing the inquiry. Understand? I could always ask you to come to the police station.'

'Oh, I just remembered,' Birgit said timidly. 'His name was Wagner. Nils Wagner.'

'And where does Nils Wagner live?'

'It was Bungalow 210 in Ruster Bay. What's he done now?'

'I can't tell you that, but you're lucky to be alive.'

Finishing the call, he dialled Olivia's number.

'I have a lead,' he said as soon as Olivia picked up. 'We need to go to Burgenland.'

'I can't get away at the moment.'

'But it's important. It's about . . .'

'Papa's not well. I need to look after him.'

'I'm so sorry.'

'I'll ring you later,' Olivia said and ended the call.

Resting his chin on his hands, Levi pondered whether he should wait for Olivia to be free or go to the bungalow by himself.

Finally, he decided he couldn't wait. Opening a drawer in the cabinet, he took out the old leather jacket lying screwed up at the bottom. Five years ago, he'd stuffed it away and sworn never to wear it again. Carefully he spread it out on his desk. He could still detect dried blood on one sleeve. When the bullet hit him in the thigh and severed the artery, Levi had tried to stop the flow with his arm. He dispelled the memory and slipped the jacket on. The leather had become brittle since he'd last worn it.

But it still fits, he thought and grabbed his car keys.

'What are you doing?' Rebecca was standing in the doorway, nervously stroking her long hair.

'I need to go out for a short while,' Levi said.

'Is that the jacket?' Rebecca said, pointing with her slender fingers.

'Yes, exactly,' Levi said. 'You need to understand, Rebecca. I can't help it.'

'You promised never to meddle with that case again.'

'Can we talk about it tonight?' Levi was begging her. 'I'll explain everything then. I simply have to do it. That much I owe Lisa.'

'As you wish. I'm disappointed you can't keep your promise, but I suppose I have to trust you. What other choice do I have?'

What was he supposed to do? Levi hated letting her down like this, but was that reason enough to leave a murder case unsolved? No, he just couldn't do it. Tight-lipped and his gut churning with guilt, Levi headed for the door. He had to see this thing through.

Lost in thought he took the southern motorway towards Lake Neusiedel in Burgenland. By the time he arrived at Ruster Bay, it was already late afternoon. He parked his car at the lakeside and walked slowly along the shore path which was flanked with tall reeds. Narrow jetties led from the water's edge to the holiday homes, which were mounted on raised wooden platforms and hardly visible from the path. Finally he found the right house and pushed his way through the reeds edging the narrow jetty.

It was a wooden house with a flat roof. The only entrance was at the back, alongside several small barred windows. Slowly Levi made his way along the narrow wooden decking surrounding the bungalow. Towards the lake the decking became wider, forming a large terrace. The house was fully glazed on that side, presumably to offer a spectacular view of the lake. The glass sliding doors were open, but he didn't see anybody. Levi stepped into the living area. On a chair lay a pair of denim shorts and a top, most likely belonging to a young girl. He noticed then the gentle sound of lapping water and turned, shielding his eyes against the setting sun. A girl in bikini bottoms and nothing else was lying on a lilo, floating on the water, her long blonde hair lifting in the breeze.

It could be Lisa, Levi thought. Maybe Olivia had been right after all to wonder whether Lisa was still alive. Maybe, being so frightened of her own father, she'd found refuge with Nils Wagner. Levi stepped out onto the terrace.

'Lisa!' he called. The girl turned around and waved. She had very delicate features and appeared very young.

'Lisa, come back to the house!' he called again. The girl turned the lilo around and paddled with both hands towards the shore. Gracefully she pulled herself up on the deck and pushed the long hair from her face. She was probably no more than fourteen and very pretty. But it wasn't Lisa.

'Hello, I am Lydia,' the girl said with a marked accent. 'You are friend of Nils?'

'Yes,' Levi answered. He was disappointed. 'Get dressed, please.' He threw a towel towards her.

'Nils likes it when I walk around naked. It is much healthier, he says.' Lydia wrapped the towel around herself.

'Where is Nils?' Levi asked.

'He has gone out to buy wine and crisps,' the girl answered. 'He will be back soon.'

'I'll wait for him inside,' Levi said, going back into the house.

There was a hint of perfume in the air when he entered the large open-plan living area. At the back were two doors, one of which led into a small bedroom. The scent was stronger here, as if the person wearing the perfume had been here a short while ago. There was a double bed, a fitted wardrobe and two wooden cubes serving as bedside tables. Next to the bed was a large mirror that didn't seem to match the rest of the interior. He stared at it, lost in thought, then he bent down. On the floor he detected faint scratches, as though the mirror had been dragged recently. Slowly Levi's fingertips felt around the rim of the mirror until he found a small button. He pressed it and the mirror slid soundlessly aside. Behind it was a small, windowless room, probably a walk-in wardrobe that had been adapted. Dozens of DVDs and photo albums sat on a shelf. A camera, mounted on a tripod, stood in the middle of the small space, the lens pointing at the bedroom. A quick look at the back of the door told Levi that this was a two-way mirror. Nils had secretly filmed his own sex games.

Carefully he took one of the photo albums. It contained pictures of very young girls, all naked and shot in sexually explicit poses. Levi flicked through the pages and then stopped short. One photo showed Lisa.

Levi was so occupied with the photos that he only heard the steps when it was too late.

'A nice collection of erotic photos, don't you think?' a voice said behind him. It could only be Nils Wagner. 'I particularly like Lydia. She looks exactly like Lisa.'

'The girl is a child,' Levi said, not turning around.

'She's like a little fairy. Hails from the Ukraine and ended up in Hungary. I brought her to Austria and she's extremely grateful.'

'But she's a minor. Sex with her is a criminal offence.'

'Only if someone reports it,' Nils retorted. 'You've entered my house without permission.'

'That's irrelevant now. When we search the house and find all this incriminating material, you'll end up in prison for sex with a minor as well as murder,' Levi said, turning round at last. Nils was leaning on the doorframe, a gun in his hand.

'What murder are you talking about?' Nils wiped the sweat from his forehead.

'The murder of Lisa Manz. You killed her.' Levi took a step towards him. 'And then you set fire to the poor girl's body.'

'Shut your mouth. You don't get it, do you?' Nils whispered hoarsely. 'What do you know about true love? The more illicit this love was, the more intensely I felt it. Those photos were taken at the height of our passion – no one could deny it – but unfortunately, Lisa's father discovered our relationship and tried to blackmail me. I was to treat Lisa with illegal hypnosis so she'd no longer be so rebellious. It was completely against my ethical values, but I didn't have a choice. Richard Manz knew too much. Richard is a psychopath who should be put away. He controls everything.' Nils pointed the gun barrel towards the photo album that Levi was still holding. 'Those photos are the evidence of our love.'

'I only see a frightened young girl being molested by you. Lisa didn't want any of that, right? But you can't accept it.'

'I did warn her about the student,' Nils said, 'but she didn't listen.'

'What was the name of that student?'

'No more questions. It won't help you now,' Nils answered angrily, shifting the gun. 'Put the album back and then get out of here. You defile the precious sanctity of this place.'

Hands above his head, Levi went back to the living room. The sun was sinking into the lake like a huge orange ball, and its light, red as blood, flooded the room.

'We'll wait until dark and then you'll go on your last journey.'

'You'd never have the guts to kill me,' Levi said, trying to think his way out of the situation. All he could hope to do was convince this madman that he understood how he might fall in love with a fourteen-year-old. 'It was like a high, wasn't it?' he continued. 'You see a young girl, beautiful and pure as angel. The father had terrorised this precious angel with sadistic games and referred her to the clinic. And then she found you there, waiting to destroy her completely.' Levi slowly lowered his arms.

'No, not to destroy Lisa, but to set her free. My God, how did it all go so wrong?' Nils whispered, raising the gun again. 'Keep your hands up.'

'If you shoot me now, how will you explain the death to the police?' Levi asked. 'And apart from that, Lydia is still here.'

'Lydia will keep her mouth shut. I could have mistaken you for a burglar.' More sweat was beading on Nils's forehead. 'I shot you in self-defence, because you threatened me.'

'Nobody will believe that.'

'It would be even better if there were no body.'

'Will you set fire to me like you did with Lisa?'

'No. I'm going to dump you in the lake.'

41

Once Olivia had sent the woman away, she dialled the number of a student nurse she knew from the clinic.

'Marie, would you mind looking after my father tonight? He's quite upset, and I don't want to leave him on his own.'

'You're in luck, Frau Doctor. I happen to be free this evening.'

Marie arrived at the flat a short time later.

'Papa, this is Marie. She'll look after you.'

Leopold nodded, still confused. 'I'm tired.'

'You can go to bed soon.'

Together with Marie she helped Leopold out of the black suit he'd put on especially for his move to the home and when the old man was finally in bed, she started to unpack the suitcases. Afterwards she carried both suitcases into her father's study then put all the files and books back on the shelves and propped up the bent stalk of the orchid with a stick. She decided that tomorrow, as soon as the flower shops opened, she'd buy another orchid for her father.

She tiptoed back to the bedroom. Marie was sitting at Leopold's bedside, engrossed in a book.

'How is he?' Olivia whispered.

'He seems quite relaxed.'

'I need to go out again. Can I leave him with you?'

'No problem, Frau Doctor. Your father's in good hands with me.'

Olivia went through to the hallway and tried calling Levi but again he didn't answer.

What did he mean when he said he had a lead? she wondered. *What lead?* She tried again, but this time his phone was switched off altogether. Olivia paced up and down the hallway, feeling increasingly anxious. *What did he mean?*

Finally she couldn't bear it any longer and dialled Levi's landline.

'Rebecca Kant,' said a soft woman's voice at the other end.

'This is Olivia Hofmann, the psychiatrist . . .'

'I know who you are,' Rebecca interrupted.

'I'm sorry to bother you, but I can't get hold of Levi on his mobile. He mentioned a trip to Burgenland. Do you know what he might have meant by that?'

'I don't deal with Levi's appointments. I'm not his secretary,' Rebecca said coldly.

'I didn't mean it like that, but do you happen to know the address he was setting off to?'

'No, and will you please excuse me now?'

'Please have a look on his desk. It's really very urgent,' Olivia implored.

'All right,' Rebecca said with a sigh.

It took a while, and Olivia was beginning to think that Rebecca had simply dropped the receiver, but then she was back.

'I found a note with an address at Lake Neusiedel,' Rebecca said, passing it on to Olivia. 'Is something wrong with Levi? Is he in danger?'

'No, don't worry. He'll be questioning a witness.'

'Levi's not with the police any more,' Rebecca said quietly. 'When he was injured so badly, I sat at his bedside for weeks. I don't want anything like that ever to happen again.'

'No reason to worry,' Olivia said, trying to reassure the other woman. 'Levi is fine.'

'I very much hope so,' Rebecca said. 'Please tell him I love him and am waiting for him.'

Rebecca put the phone down and Olivia remained still for a few seconds, not quite sure what to do.

'How do I get to the Burgenland?' Olivia didn't own a car, and it was already late afternoon. She toyed with the idea of postponing the journey to the next day, but she was too worried. No, she needed to find out what had happened. After a moment's hesitation, she dialled Simon Berger's number. 'Hi, Simon, it's me, Olivia.'

'Olivia, what a surprise!' Simon sounded genuinely pleased. 'Shall we meet up? Listen, I'm sorry about what I said the other evening. You know, my inappropriate questioning.'

'Forget it,' Olivia answered. 'Can you drive me to Lake Neusiedel in the Burgenland?'

'Of course. Sunset by Lake Neusiedel. How very romantic.' Simon sounded genuinely enthusiastic.

'No, I'm only asking you for a lift.' Olivia stopped him in his tracks. 'I'm looking for someone. Can you do me this favour?'

'Oh, that's a shame. And here was I thinking you were inviting me to a romantic dinner by the lakeside.'

'Yes or no?' Olivia said in response. She had no intention of flirting with Simon Berger.

'Yes, of course. I can do that. Shall I pick you up at home? In about ten minutes?'

'No, I'm in the Ninth District with my father.' Olivia gave him the address.

A quarter of an hour later a four-wheel drive stopped in front of the house. Simon jumped from the driver's seat and rang the bell.

'It took a bit longer. The traffic,' he apologised as Olivia met him at the door.

'Nice motor. Must have cost a bomb,' Olivia said, looking at the car.

'Well, it belongs to a friend and it's over five years old, but it drives OK.' He patted the bonnet as if it were a horse.

'Did you have an accident?' Olivia asked casually, pointing to a long scratch on the wing.

'Happened a few days ago when I was parking,' Simon said coolly. Then he bent down to whisper in Olivia's ear, 'I'm not that interested in cars.'

'Good for you,' Olivia said. Michael had been obsessed with the damn things. 'How about gambling?' she asked.

'Gambling? What do you mean?' Simon looked at her uncomprehendingly.

'Well, games. With dice or cards and things.'

'No, that's not my thing. Why do you ask?'

'Oh, nothing. Don't know what I was thinking,' Olivia said evasively. She was still paying off Michael's gambling debts. 'Come on, let's go.'

While they were threading through the late afternoon rush-hour traffic, Simon told her about his work at the clinic.

'So why did you choose the psychiatric clinic for your stint as a junior doctor?' Olivia asked. 'Do you want to specialise in psychiatry later? You'll earn a lot of money as a consultant.'

'I don't really care about money,' Simon said, looking straight ahead. 'I want to help people suffering from mental illness.'

'That's rare among young people,' Olivia said. 'Most of them are after a lot of money and as fast as possible.'

'Well, I'm different,' Simon said. He shot her a swift glance. 'Would you accept me as your patient?'

'You mean for me to act as your psychiatrist?'

'Exactly.'

'Well, why not. Do you have problems with your girlfriends?' Olivia asked ironically.

'No, but please do consider me as your patient.' Simon held his hand towards her. 'Agreed?'

'You'll have to sign a declaration of consent first,' Olivia said, finding the situation increasingly strange.

'Do you have a form on you?' Simon flicked the indicator and pulled up on the hard shoulder. 'I'll sign it right now, this minute.'

'What's the matter, Simon?' Olivia asked, folding her hands in her lap.

'I'll only talk once I'm your patient.'

'OK. Consider this as the declaration of consent,' Olivia said, pulling a creased scrap of paper from her bag. Simon signed it without looking, then put his foot down and carried on towards Lake Neusiedel.

'Five years ago, I helped Lisa Manz escape from the clinic,' he said. 'I was a student at the time and got to know her as my patient. I felt sorry for her. Her father bullied her, but at the clinic she was treated by Nils Wagner. That was like jumping from the frying pan into the fire. I had to help her.'

'Why didn't you tell all this to the police at the time?' Olivia began to see Simon through new eyes. His face was screwed up, and he was clenching the steering wheel so tight that his knuckles had gone white.

'If I'd admitted to it, they'd have fired me. I'd have lost my place at med school, and I couldn't risk that.'

'You'll have to talk to the police,' Olivia insisted, 'or shall I do it for you?'

184

'As my psychiatrist, you're bound by confidentiality,' Simon reminded her. 'You're not allowed to say anything.' With a determined expression, Simon drove faster. 'I took Lisa to a derelict house – she was to wait there until they gave up searching for her. After that I planned to take her abroad. She'd have been safe from Nils and her father.'

'So you were the last person to see Lisa alive?'

'No. The last person was Lisa's murderer.'

42

LISA'S DIARY

The student turns up in my room in the middle of the night. Suddenly he's standing next to my bed, looking at me in a strange way. I wince.

'Quiet!' he says and puts a hand to my mouth. 'You want to get out of here, don't you?'

'Yes,' I breathe when he takes his hand away, 'that's what I want. What Nils is doing to me is disgusting. He wants more and more.' And then I tell him everything. I want the student to listen to me.

'OK, OK,' he interrupts. 'I understand – that's why I'm here. Get dressed,' he tells me.

'Where are you taking me?'

'To a safe place. Nobody will look for you there. Then we'll see,' he whispers. 'Hurry up.'

I throw on my clothes, grab my rucksack.

'You can't take that rucksack.'

'But I need it.'

'OK, if you must.'

We sneak out of my room into the corridor. The student knows where the surveillance cameras are, and we stick close to the walls. I can see the reception desk through the glass door. A nurse is reading a newspaper.

'Wait,' he whispers. It's strange but the door's open – normally it's locked. He seems relieved. Now only the nurse is in our way. We duck behind a laundry trolley and wait. The student grabs my hand. I feel more hopeful.

Finally, the nurse gets up and disappears into another room. The student rushes through the foyer and bends down over the reception desk. I follow him and see that he's looking for something. Silently the large entrance doors open. My way to freedom.

'Run, take the steps. Wait in the car park,' he whispers and turns back to the desk. 'I have to reactivate the lock on the door.'

I run down the steps, my heart pounding like mad. There are still people who actually want to help me. I'm not alone in the world.

The car park is dark, and I crouch, slipping from car to car all the way to the entrance. The porter has nodded off and in the shadow of his cabin I can avoid the cameras. Then I'm out of the grounds of the clinic altogether. I wait for what seems an eternity until finally the student turns up. He simply went through the main entrance.

'My nightshift is over,' he says and pulls a pack of cigarettes from his pocket. He takes one out and offers it to me.

'Here, have one, it'll calm you down,' he says.

He lights it for me and I inhale, which makes me cough. He laughs and pats my shoulder. I turn round once more and see the nurse by the window. Did she see us? Who cares now in any case?

'Come on.' He pulls me along behind him.

Silently we walk the night streets. I feel happy and protected for the first time. I take the student's arm and feel safe. The area is getting darker and most of the windows are barred and boarded, shops seem empty. We stop in front of an old grey house.

'Here we are,' says the student and kicks the door open. It's cold and very dark inside. He takes my hand and leads me to a set of steps.

'We'll go down to the cellar,' he says. 'Don't be afraid.'

'I'm not afraid as long as you're with me,' I whisper, grabbing his hand even tighter.

'Good, good.' He leads me through a maze of cellar rooms. 'Nearly there.'

Then he stops in front of a wooden partition.

'Well, this is it. It's not very comfortable, but you'll be safe here for a while.'

'It's so dark,' I say. I'm growing anxious.

'There's no light,' says the student, 'but I've brought a mattress and some blankets for you.'

'Why are you so good to me?' I ask and turn away, so he doesn't see my tears.

'You should have a chance for a normal life.'

Then he grabs my shoulders, turns me around and shines the torch in my face.

'You'll have to be really brave now, Lisa.'

43

Simon stopped the car in a car park near Ruster Bay and leaned over to Olivia.

'I can rely on your absolute discretion, can't I?'

'I want to get out.' Olivia rattled the door handle, but the door remained locked.

'The child lock is activated,' Simon said. 'When is my next appointment with you?' he asked. 'We have a doctor–patient relationship now, don't we?'

'Yes. Call me about an appointment,' Olivia replied nervously. The door clicked as it unlocked, and she opened it hastily and climbed out. Leaning against the car, she took a deep breath. How should she deal with this? Simon was right – she was bound by medical confidentiality. Had he really been telling the truth? His behaviour had been more than strange. Simon wasn't the charming young man she'd seen before. He also had a dark side.

'Is this the place you wanted to go to?' Simon's voice came from behind her.

Olivia turned to see him leaning against the car too, his hands in the pockets of his jeans. The last rays of sun were illuminating the reeds on the bank, swaying in the breeze. Olivia looked around.

There were only a few cars. Suddenly she saw Levi's white convertible. With the hood up, it looked different, which was why she'd not spotted it straight away.

'Yes, this is the right place. You can go back now. I'm expected here.'

'As you wish.' Simon sounded disappointed, but then he went back to the driver's side and got in. 'Look after yourself, Olivia,' he called through the open window.

'Thank you so much for bringing me here,' Olivia said. 'And do show your friend the scratch.'

'I'll tell Tesi.' Simon waved again, and then the four-wheel drive disappeared in the light of the sinking sun.

Olivia set off along the small wooden walkway towards the bungalow. The wind rose and the reeds were now rustling menacingly in the breeze. She could hear two voices inside, muffled by the sounds around her. Creeping closer, she listened carefully.

'I loved Lisa and gave her the precious pendant, which was a family heirloom. My grandmother would never have forgiven me for that, but the things you do for love . . .' It was Nils's voice, there was no doubt about it. Suddenly everything made sense.

'What is this love you keep referring to? You abused Lisa, and when the girl wanted to report you to the police, you killed her. But you'll be called to account for that now.' Amid the rustling and the wind, she recognised Levi's distinct voice.

'I adored her. I wanted to start a new life with her.'

'With a fourteen-year-old girl? You're talking rubbish. You only used her to feed your dirty fantasies.'

'Of course our love was impossible. I knew that.' Nils's voice now sounded resigned. 'But here, in this house, we at least had an illusion of happiness.'

'I cannot even begin to imagine that a young girl would feel that kind of love.'

'And what do you know about love?' Nils hissed contemptuously. 'Of course, it was slightly different for me than it was for Lisa. I knew our love was forbidden and tried to suppress it, but my feelings for her were too strong.'

'And that's why you killed her,' Olivia heard Levi say.

'Stop saying that!' Nils shrieked, his voice cracking. It sounded as if he was about to have a nervous breakdown. 'It was horrendous when she died.'

'Was that a confession?' Levi asked, but Nils kept silent.

As silently as she could, Olivia tiptoed along the wooden walls of the bungalow to gain a view inside.

'You killed Lisa. It's time to confess.' Levi's voice sounded hard and determined, as if there was no way he'd be tolerating any contradiction.

'Shut up or I'll kill you.'

Olivia froze and held her breath. In panic she pondered how she could possibly help Levi. While she was looking around for a weapon, a shot rang out through the evening air. A few storks flew up in panic.

'Levi, what happened?' cried Olivia, running along the decking now to the terrace. The large glass doors were wide open, but she was blinded by the sun and all she could see was the silhouette of a man sitting on the floor, his legs spread wide, his back to the wall. A handgun lay on the floor next to him.

'Oh my God!' She dropped her bag and ran into the living room, stopping short in front of the person on the floor. The man's face was gone. Brain tissue and splinters of bone were spread all over the wall behind him. Olivia retched, then jumped when a hand fell on her shoulder.

'Don't look at him, Olivia.'

With a choked cry, she whirled around to face Levi. 'Oh my God, I'm so happy it isn't you,' she whispered, flinging her arms around him. 'I heard you talking and then the shot. I was so afraid.'

'It's over.' Levi pushed her gently out onto the terrace.

'Is it Nils?' Olivia asked, glancing back into the living room over Levi's shoulder.

'Yes. Nils Wagner has just shot himself in front of me,' Levi said softly, then took out his mobile and dialled a number.

'Hello, Reiter, Levi here. It looks like Lisa Manz's murderer has just shot himself.' He ended the call and went outside to Olivia.

'You're not allowed to go inside. It's a crime scene now.'

'Tell me what happened,' Olivia asked quietly.

By the time Inspector Reiter and the local police arrived, Levi had already told Olivia about the secret room in the bungalow. The young girl who had run from the house had been picked up in the village and taken to the police station. Numb with shock and exhaustion, Olivia sat on the terrace with a cup of tea a policewoman brought to her. She watched indifferently as two men carried Nils's body away in a metal coffin.

'Frau Doctor Hofmann. Did you actually hear Nils Wagner confess to the murder of Lisa Manz?' Inspector Reiter stood in front of her, holding an old-fashioned notebook.

'Yes, I think so. It all happened very quickly. Nils kept saying how much he'd loved Lisa, but that it had been a forbidden love. Her death had been a terrible shock for him.' Olivia tried to remember the exact words of the dialogue she'd overheard, but only came up with fragments.

'Her death had been terrible for him? Are you quite sure?' Reiter asked as he perched in front of her on the wooden planks. 'That sounds like a confession.'

'I just don't know any more, but I think so.' Olivia found it hard to express herself. She didn't want to talk or think any more, just sleep.

'Thank you,' Reiter said, closing his notebook. 'I reckon we've finally solved the Lisa Manz case.'

44

LISA'S DIARY

I'm waiting in the dark. It's raining outside and I can hear the monotonous dripping on the cobblestones in the backyard. Something dark scurries past me. A rat.

'I've brought you something to eat.' The student turns up, and I sigh with relief.

'I want to get out of here,' I say, sniffing noisily. 'I need to get outside.'

'That's not possible just yet. The police are looking for you. They even showed your photo on TV.' The student is stressed.

When the light from the torch falls on his face, I see red patches on his cheeks.

'I didn't think they'd conduct a nationwide search – the whole of Austria is looking for you. I'm getting nervous,' he mumbles. 'It was a stupid idea to get you out of the clinic.'

'But you saved me. I'll be grateful to you for the rest of my life!'

'No one must ever know that it was me who helped you. Do you understand?'

'Sure. Can you just hold me now? That'll give me the strength to stay here and wait.'

'All right. Come here.' The student spreads his arms and embraces me. I feel his warm body, raise my head and kiss him on the lips.

'What if we fall in love with each other?'

At the same moment I hear a sound from the back of the cellar. It's a slow tapping noise, enhanced by the ceiling and echoing all around us. The noise gets louder and louder and grows gradually more threatening. I cling even tighter to the student.

'What's that? Please don't leave me – I'm so frightened!'

'It's just some stray cats. They're hunting mice,' he reassures me.

'But it sounded like steps. Maybe there's someone else in the cellar?'

'And who would that be? The house is condemned. Nobody lives here. Don't worry.' The student gives me a fleeting kiss on the forehead. 'I have to go now.'

'Please stay a little while longer,' I implore him but he shakes his head.

'I'll be back tomorrow,' he says as a goodbye. 'Try to sleep.'

The light from his torch dances over the walls like a will-o'-the-wisp. Thick darkness is sinking down on me like a suffocating pillow. I find it hard to breathe. My heart is pounding as if it's about to burst. I'm nearly blind with fear and try and scribble in my diary to calm myself.

I wake in the middle of the night and sit bolt upright on my mattress. Again I hear the tapping. It's more like a pattering. In panic I grab the pendant the doctor gave me.

Rather than reassuring me it seems to have the opposite effect. Frantically I tear the leather strap from my neck and shove it in my rucksack. This amulet attracts evil, and I regret not having thrown it away.

The pattering doesn't stop. Instead, it's coming closer. And it's not a cat. Somebody's sneaking towards the wooden partition.

45

Olivia sat in a vegan restaurant in the Second District and waited for Levi. All the papers had headlined with the news of Nils Wagner's suicide. A renowned psychiatrist who had abused underage girls in a holiday cottage was a big story, even more so during the silly season of the summer months. Olivia had refused to talk to the press but gave one exclusive interview to her journalist friend, Anna, in which she detailed her side of the story. That Nils had had a fatal preference for very young girls was considered fact, but Olivia still could not see Nils as a cold-blooded murderer. Since the events in the Burgenland, she'd only talked to Levi briefly on the phone. He'd gone off on a long holiday with Rebecca. Today they'd arranged to meet for lunch to discuss the whole affair.

'Nice to see you,' Olivia heard Levi call from behind her. She'd been lost in her thoughts and not noticed him coming in.

'Hi, Levi,' Olivia said, getting up to give him a friendly peck on the cheek. He was tanned and looked decidedly relaxed. The deep furrows on his forehead had disappeared, and she realised he was quite good-looking.

'How was your holiday?' she asked after they'd ordered.

'I have a feeling that things between Rebecca and me will get back to how they were before,' Levi said carefully, 'but it'll take a while. We'd grown quite estranged and I only really noticed it over the course of this holiday. Anyway, how about you? How's your father?' he asked, trying to change the subject.

'Papa has a full-time person to take care of him now. I see him in the evenings.'

'Isn't that still quite demanding? Shuttling between your two flats every day?'

'I've moved in with him,' Olivia said, chewing on a piece of tofu.

'Oh,' Levi said, with a grimace. 'Of course, it's a big flat. You can have your own space.'

'It's not forever,' Olivia replied, 'but I've had to scale back my expenses in order to afford someone to look after him and the medication.'

'Don't overdo it,' Levi warned her.

'It's fine. So how about your cabinet with all the files?'

'I took it to the dump, and the files all went into the shredder.'

'Right. You know, one thing still bothers me,' Olivia said.

'And what's that?' Levi leaned across the table.

'Why did Jonathan tell me in his last session that Lisa had come back?'

'Do you still think that Lisa could have faked her own death to escape Nils and her father?'

'I'm just thinking aloud but it is possible. I can't imagine Nils killing the object of his desire and then setting fire to her.'

Levi frowned. 'I did discuss that with Reiter. There's the dental evidence, although someone could have tampered with it. If not her, then who was the dead girl?'

'One of the nameless girls, maybe, like the one you met in Nils's house?'

'Possibly, but then who was the person Jonathan claimed to have seen?'

'Well, he could have been mistaken.'

'But he took a photo. I saw it. It could have been Lisa.'

'Shame we never found Jonathan's mobile.'

'But I still have a copy.' Olivia remembered the photo that had been sent to her anonymously. All of a sudden she couldn't bear to sit still any longer. 'Come on, let's go to my flat and we'll have a look at it.'

They paid the bill and went out to Levi's car. A short while later they arrived at Olivia's father's flat.

'Go on through to the living room. I'll just say hello to my father,' she said. Just as she said this, the door to Leopold's room opened and the old man came out.

'Olivia, Michael, how nice to see you. Where is my little Juli?' he asked, then looked at Levi searchingly. 'The beard suits you, Michael.'

'Papa, this is Levi, a friend of mine.'

'Michael won't like that,' Leopold replied. The day nurse came through from the kitchen.

'Your father is well today, nearly his old self. Come on, Leopold, it's time for your afternoon nap,' she said gently, taking the old man's arm to lead him back to his room.

'A difficult situation for you,' Levi said, once they were finally parked in front of Olivia's laptop in the living room.

'I take it as it comes,' Olivia said, although she didn't look very happy. 'Here's the photo anyway.'

The image of the person was blurry and not easy to identify.

'Can you enlarge it?' Levi asked.

'Yup.' Olivia zoomed the image closer, but it only became more blurred.

'It's just not good enough,' Levi said in resigned tones, 'but maybe someone can help us with it.' He got his mobile out and punched in a number. A male voice answered, and Levi described the problem. He gave Olivia the email address, and she sent the picture.

'Can you send it back as soon as possible, mate?' Levi asked and put the mobile back into his pocket. 'We'll have to wait a moment.'

The return email came through a short while later.

'It's the photo,' she said, opening the attachment. The image was still quite blurred, but it was clearer now that it was a woman whose face was visible in profile.

'It could be Lisa,' Levi said as he zoomed in.

'Which means that Lisa faked her own death,' Olivia said excitedly.

'Wait.' Levi leaned forward and squinted at it. 'There's something about this photo but I can't quite put my finger on it.' He leaned back and closed his eyes.

Olivia looked at him curiously. What had he seen? What was unusual about the photo? The enlargement showed a heavily pixelated face, but one could detect blonde hair and Lisa's delicate features. It was possible that it was her.

Then all of a sudden Levi opened his eyes wide and rapped on the desk. 'I've just worked out what's been bothering me. Bring the laptop,' he said to Olivia. 'We need to leave this minute.'

'Where are we going?' Olivia looked at Levi in surprise.

'You'll see.'

46

Dark clouds were blotting out the sun and it looked like rain, when Levi stopped his Saab in front of the extravagant gate and mumbled something into the intercom. The gate slid open, and he raced up the long and winding drive.

'You think Lisa is hiding at her parents' house?' Olivia looked at Levi, doubt in her eyes.

'Wait and see,' he said, stopping the car and getting out. Olivia followed with her laptop. A mountain bike leaned against a nearby wall, a helmet dangling from the handlebars. Next to it sat a black four-wheel drive that Olivia seemed to recognise. As before, Theresa Manz was waiting for them on the front steps. The wind was blowing her blonde hair into her face, and from a distance she looked like a young girl.

'Did you miss me?' she asked Levi ironically.

'I just want to show you something,' Levi said, ignoring her question.

'Oh, how exciting,' Theresa said, turning her back on him. They went into the large drawing room, and Olivia put her laptop on the table.

'I'm going to show you a photo, and you need to tell me whether or not you recognise the person in it,' Levi said, opening up the laptop.

'And if I refuse to do that?' Theresa looked provocatively from Levi to Olivia. 'What does our psychiatrist have to say about this? Isn't it a bit . . . manipulative? Am I being forced to identify someone?'

'Don't exaggerate,' Olivia said. 'It's a simple request.'

'OK, show me the photo.'

Levi turned the laptop so she could see the screen while Olivia watched Theresa's expression closely. She barely glanced at the photo before turning the laptop back to Levi. Her face hardened, and it seemed as if a barrier had gone up behind her eyes.

'I'm sorry, I don't know this woman. Who's it supposed to be?'

'You.'

'Me? You must be completely off your head.' Theresa leaned back on the sofa and looked at Olivia as if for help. 'Say something – do I really have to put up with this?'

'Are you the woman in the photo?' Again Olivia studied Theresa's face and body language, noticing how Theresa swallowed and touched her hair.

'That's not me.'

'Yes, it most clearly is you!' Levi said. 'See the little fleck right there?' He pointed to a black dot on the woman's face.

'What, that? It's a fly. A dirty lens. It could be anything,' Theresa said, but Olivia noticed that her voice had started to tremble. Suddenly the woman seemed like a cornered animal.

'It's a mole. And you have exactly the same mole with three points on your own cheek,' Levi said calmly. 'How did you know about the derelict house and Lisa's rucksack?'

'What does it matter? There's no evidence.' Theresa pulled her legs up and sat huddled on the broad sofa. 'I watched them,' she whispered. 'He'd hidden her in that cellar. And then he kissed her. It was disgusting – we'd been in love for two years. We'd made plans for a life together. And then suddenly he wanted to leave me.'

'Who wanted to leave you?' Olivia asked gently, trying not to irritate Theresa.

'Simon, the junior doctor. He was a student at the time. I met him on one of my visits to the clinic. We had an affair for two years. It was heaven on earth for me – at last someone loved me. But Simon was just as mad about Lisa as Nils was. The little slut destroyed my entire life.'

A door opened, and Simon entered.

'What are you talking about? It was a mistake, Theresa – a terrible mistake. I only wanted to help your daughter. I felt sorry for her, that was all,' Simon said. His face pale, he stared at Theresa in disgust, barely able to control himself. 'I never had an affair with Lisa. Was it you? Did you kill Lisa? Your own daughter? You're evil – and to think I once loved you!'

'Do you still love me?' Theresa asked.

'How can I love someone who's capable of something so dreadful?' Simon said coldly.

'What are you doing here, Simon?' Olivia asked. 'Are you part of this?'

'No, I came to talk to Theresa about Lisa's father. His sadistic behaviour caused Lisa's distress in the first place, but Theresa allegedly doesn't know anything about it. She doesn't even know that Lisa kept a diary.'

'It was you who sent me the pages from the diary, wasn't it?' Olivia said.

'Yes, I wanted you to keep on searching for the truth,' Simon said.

'Do you admit to having killed your own daughter out of jealousy?' Levi asked Theresa. 'How could you be so cruel?'

'Pah, it's exactly the opposite – I have too many feelings. I only wanted to be loved. When nobody loves you, you start hating. Medea also killed her children out of revenge.'

'We're not in the theatre. This is real life.'

'Real life! In my reality I loved my daughter. "We look like sisters", I often said, when we were standing in front of a mirror together. But she didn't want a sister, she wanted a mother, and yet I never had motherly feelings for her.'

'Did you also kill Jonathan Stade?' Olivia said, interrupting Theresa's self-pitying monologue.

'Yes. Is that the name of that awful man? I forgot his name immediately. He was a stalker and watched Lisa in her cellar. And then he saw me too when I went there to confront her.'

She jumped up from the sofa suddenly and went over towards a large mirror hanging over the sideboard.

'Why are you taking Simon away from me? You've already destroyed my career. Your father spends his whole time thinking up ways to control you and completely ignores me. And then you have the nerve to take away my lover. I can't let that happen.'

Theresa talked to her mirror image as if it was really Lisa in the reflection. Then she turned around again. Olivia got the impression that Theresa was enjoying her performance as if she were on stage and they were the audience.

'I told Lisa she was evil, but she just cried. She wanted me to feel sorry for her. She clung to me and whined *Mama, Mama*. So I pushed her away. She fell and hit her head on one of the stone steps. It was a nasty fall and she died on the spot. It was an accident – you must believe me. Jonathan saw and tried to blackmail me. I gave him money, but during his sessions with you he must have discovered his conscience.' She scowled at Olivia. 'He'd have told you everything. I had to prevent that and pushed him out of the window. It's all Lisa's fault. She destroyed our family.'

With Theresa still reciting her monologue, for all the world as if she were in a theatre, Levi got up and called the police.

'You've kept your ghastly secret for a long time,' he said, 'but the police are on their way. It's time for the truth to come out now. The press will also be arriving shortly.'

'The press?' Theresa raised her chin. 'And television cameras as well?' she asked. 'My God, I need to do my make-up. How do I look?' She glanced around.

'Like a murderess,' Levi snapped.

'Shut up!' Theresa clapped her hands over her ears. 'I'll make it to the front pages. I'll be famous – finally famous! This is my last great performance.'

47

The cemetery in Döbling was like an oasis of peace on the outskirts of the hectic city of Vienna. A number of celebrities such as the actor Josef Kainz, and the father of the state of Israel, Theodor Herzl, had found their final resting place here. But it was also the last refuge of her mother, Flora, and since Leopold was no longer able to look after her grave, Olivia had taken on the task.

On a hot summer's day Olivia walked along the main avenue, shaded by old trees. She stopped in front of her mother's simple grave and noticed some fresh flowers in a vase. It was a bunch of wildflowers like the ones her daughter Juli had loved so much. Who could have brought them? Olivia sat down on the bench opposite the grave, lost in thought.

It was very quiet here, and Olivia relaxed. From where she sat, she had a good view of the main gates and the side entrance. A man and a little girl, maybe ten or eleven years old, were walking slowly towards the exit. Olivia couldn't help watching them, painfully reminded of her own family. The man had long fair hair, while the girl's darker hair was in two plaits. Shortly before the gate, the girl suddenly turned around and waved to Olivia.

'Juli!' Olivia shouted, jumping up. The man heard her and was startled, grabbing the girl by the hand and walking on hurriedly.

'Michael! Juli!' Olivia ran after them, her voice breaking with excitement. Panting, she arrived at the gate and scanned both sides of the road but there was no one in sight. A car turned out of the car park and raced past her. For a fraction of a second Olivia saw the girl's face looking at her through the back window. She had Olivia's dark hair and light grey eyes.

There was no mistake. She wasn't wrong – the girl in the car was her daughter. It was Juli.

'Juli!' she called out again and ran after the car, but the driver increased his speed, and soon it was only a dark spot in the distance. Eventually it disappeared.

Olivia crouched down by the side of the road and buried her face in her hands. Her heart was bursting but she couldn't cry. There was only a huge vacuum inside. A vacuum that grew larger until there was no more room for feeling or sensation.

After a while she got up and went back to the cemetery where she'd parked her bicycle. She couldn't undo the padlock because her hands were shaking so violently. She had to lean against a wall and take several deep breaths, try to think clearly and approach the incident rationally. Why would they be in this cemetery today of all days? But then she remembered that it would have been Flora's birthday. Had she really seen her daughter and her husband?

Olivia lifted her head and closed her eyes. The warmth of the sun on her skin calmed her and she knew what she had to do. Taking her mobile from her bag, she started to pace up and down. What would he think of her? Would he consider her mad if she rang and told him what had just happened? *Whatever*, she thought, and dialled his number. The phone rang for a while, and Olivia was about to give up when she heard his voice. Before he could say much more, she told him everything.

48

Levi Kant walked across the windswept concrete of the Praterstern. He was holding a bunch of flowers like so often before, but this time he'd place them at the foot of the crumbling concrete wall not in memory of the shooting, but in memory of Lisa Manz. Lisa's murderess had been caught, and now he could finally let it go and concentrate on his relationship. Rebecca had suffered because of his obsession but things would change. He'd be there for his wife and encourage her to trust her talent as a pianist. Maybe someday with his help she'd have the confidence to perform again.

Placing the flowers on the ground, he straightened, folded his arms across his chest and stared down at them; the flowers provided the only colour in this concrete desert. He stood there for a while, thinking over the events of the past few weeks. He'd not seen Olivia since their visit to the Manz house and he wondered how her father was. Sometime at the end of the summer, he'd meet up with her to talk over everything that had happened. No trial date had been set yet for Theresa Manz because her barristers were pleading mental incapacity. Now it was in the hands of experts, and Theresa had been placed in a secure ward. One thing she had achieved – she'd been front-page news in all the papers and magazines as the 'Mother from Hell'.

Theresa had also confessed to the attempted murder of Olivia Hofmann with her car. In the case of Jonathan Stade she had mixed a cocktail of drugs and forced him to drink it. Jonathan's senses had been numbed and it had been easy to push him from the window. All of this Theresa reported to the prosecution service as if describing a new theatrical role, although she never said a word about how she'd managed to bring Lisa's body to the quarry in Sankt Margarethen. Her former lover Simon Berger became a suspect, of course, but he had an alibi. Levi didn't care – the murder of Lisa Manz had been solved, and that was all that mattered to him.

'I hope you fare better in another world, Lisa,' he said quietly, thinking of the sad girl who'd led such a tragic and horrible life.

At that moment his mobile rang, chasing away his maudlin thoughts.

'Hello, Olivia,' he said in surprise. He'd not expected to hear from her.

'You need to come. Right this second. I saw Michael and Juli!' she said. She was out of breath. She hadn't even said hello first.

'Easy, easy. What are you saying? Please tell me, but one thing at a time.' Levi crossed the windswept square to sit on a bench, listening carefully to what Olivia told him. 'Maybe they just looked similar. You could be mistaken,' he said, trying to calm her.

'Juli waved at me. I'm not mistaken. Will you help me – please?'

Levi hesitated, but only for a moment. He knew Olivia well by now and that she'd never give up searching for her husband and daughter.

'Where are you now?'

'At the cemetery.' Olivia told him the address.

'Wait there. I'll come over.'

Levi put his mobile away and headed off for his white Saab, which was parked on the other side of the square. Before he reached it, he turned around one last time. The wind had swept the flowers a little further away, but they remained a solitary dot of colour in the grey square. That was a good sign. Folding back the roof of the car, he climbed in. He had intended to go home and cook dinner. For a few seconds his fingers drummed on the steering wheel, undecided.

Then he started the car and drove off.

ABOUT THE AUTHORS

After more than twenty years in marketing and advertising, Barbara and Christian Schiller now live and work in Vienna and Mallorca.

They publish their gripping crime novels under the name B.C. Schiller. The team has written some of the most successful crime novels in the German language, enthralling more than 1.5 million readers.

About the Translator

Annette Charpentier, PhD, has worked as a translator for over thirty years and has translated over 250 works of fiction and non-fiction, both from German into English and from English into German.

Born in Germany, she moved to Wales thirty-five years ago.